AGE OF

CONAN™

HYBORIAN ADVENTURES

MARAUDERS
Volume II

WINDS OF
THE WILD SEA

Jeff Mariotte

ACE BOOKS, NEW YORK

THE BERKLEY PUBLISHING GROUP
Published by the Penguin Group
Penguin Group (USA) Inc.
375 Hudson Street, New York, New York 10014, USA
Penguin Group (Canada), 90 Eglinton Avenue East, Suite 700, Toronto, Ontario M4P 2Y3, Canada
(a division of Pearson Penguin Canada Inc.)
Penguin Books Ltd., 80 Strand, London WC2R 0RL, England
Penguin Group Ireland, 25 St. Stephen's Green, Dublin 2, Ireland (a division of Penguin Books Ltd.)
Penguin Group (Australia), 250 Camberwell Road, Camberwell, Victoria 3124, Australia
(a division of Pearson Australia Group Pty. Ltd.)
Penguin Books India Pvt. Ltd., 11 Community Centre, Panchsheel Park, New Delhi—110 017, India
Penguin Group (NZ), Cnr. Airborne and Rosedale Roads, Albany, Auckland 1310, New Zealand
(a division of Pearson New Zealand Ltd.)
Penguin Books (South Africa) (Pty.) Ltd., 24 Sturdee Avenue, Rosebank, Johannesburg 2196, South
Africa

Penguin Books Ltd., Registered Offices: 80 Strand, London WC2R 0RL, England

This is a work of fiction. Names, characters, places, and incidents either are the product of the author's
imagination or are used fictitiously, and any resemblance to actual persons, living or dead, business es-
tablishments, events, or locales is entirely coincidental. The publisher does not have any control over
and does not assume any responsibility for author or third-party websites or their content.

WINDS OF THE WILD SEA

An Ace Book / published by arrangement with Conan Properties International, LLC.

PRINTING HISTORY
Ace edition / April 2006

Copyright © 2006 by Conan Properties International, LLC.
Cover art by Justin Sweet.
Interior text design by Stacy Irwin.

ISBN: 0-441-01386-4

ACE
Ace Books are published by The Berkley Publishing Group,
a division of Penguin Group (USA) Inc.,
375 Hudson Street, New York, New York 10014.
ACE and the "A" design are trademarks belonging to Penguin Group (USA) Inc.

PRINTED IN THE UNITED STATES OF AMERICA

10 9 8 7 6 5 4 3 2 1

Acknowledgments

Thanks to all the people who helped make this book happen, including the gangs at Conan Properties and Ace Books, my family and friends, and the dedicated booksellers everywhere who have the most important job of all—making sure people get to see it!

PARTHENIA

KHITAI

VILAYET SEA

HYRKANIA

ISLE OF
THE SEVEN
SEA-GAVES

KUSAN

ZAMORA

KHAURAN

TURAN

VENDHYA

KOSALA

MISTY
ISLES

...S OF
...ARL

SOUTHERN SEA

1

TORCHES MOUNTED ON the dock's pilings flickered and leapt in the breeze that blew in off the Western Ocean. Moonlight silvered the tips of the choppy sea. Bare-chested Stygians worked in the night air, making a sleek black galley ready to sail. None of them knew who would travel on the dark craft. But they all knew enough to know not to ask questions about it. There were things, they understood, that it was better not to show any curiosity about, especially where the sons of the snake god Set were involved. When the ship was ready, three men in long, black robes emerged from the benighted shadows and strode silently up the gangplank.

When they boarded, no sane man wanted to stay on the ship. It was as if the three acolytes went about surrounded by a miasma of terror that drove all others away. The last man on board, high in the riggings making fast the black vertical mainsail, felt the presence of the three dark figures below. He rushed through his last knot and dove into the water rather than step onto the deck with them for even a second.

As he climbed out of the warm water and onto the dock, the other workers stood watching the ship. They were sure that it would go nowhere. All the winds were blowing in off the sea, and, although the ship was a bireme, the three had no galley slaves on board to row them out. But when one of them released the last line holding ship to dock, the ship began to drift away from shore, in spite of the waves that should have been pushing it back. To everyone's astonishment, the sails filled with wind that no one on land could feel—wind that seemed to be blowing off the shore and out toward empty sea, a complete reversal of the breezes all had felt during the course of their work. The sleek ship cut swiftly through the water, and within minutes it was out of sight, black on black.

No ship had ever sailed so rapidly, the men on the dock knew.

At least, not without help.

IN ALL OF his sixteen years, Kral had never seen so much armor.

Back home, the Pictish men fought naked, or wearing a loincloth. And the settlers they battled mostly wore leathers or buckskins, sometimes combined with shirts of mail.

But here in Tarantia, sitting on the ground looking up at Aquilonian soldiers, he saw breastplates of solid steel. Most were plain, but a couple had designs worked into the metal, the same lion insignia that showed on Aquilonian flags.

He couldn't help wondering how strong the steel was. Could a knife pierce it? An arrow? How did a man walk upright with so much weight on his shoulders, instead of on all fours like a tortoise in its shell? And how could any force stand up to an army so protected?

It looked like he might find out.

Three Rangers on one side of him—men who had fought against Picts, and hated them. Seven soldiers on the other side—more of them, better armed and armored, but men who still stared in amazement that a young Pict was sprawled in the street before them.

He picked the Rangers. They and their kind, after all, had slaughtered his clan. He owed them.

His knife had slid a couple of feet away when he had fallen. He still clutched the sword borrowed from Alanya's friend Cheveray. But a sword was an unfamiliar weapon to Kral, one he had little experience fighting with. His opponents had stopped far enough back to give him some time to make his move. Keeping his eyes trained on the soldiers, he sprang and twisted, like a cat turning to land on its feet. He scooped up the knife, feinted once toward the soldiers, then propelled himself backward, at the last minute turning again. He had fixed the positions of the three Rangers in his mind. When he could see them again, he found that none of them had moved far from where they had been.

He landed between the two on his right side. One of them was in motion toward him with his sword out, point first. Kral flicked his sword's blade at that one, to hold him at bay. The second still gawped at Kral, surprised that he was so near. As Kral had hoped, the Rangers had been certain he would go toward the soldiers.

Kral dodged the first one's blade and charged the second. This one raised a sword, but too slowly. Kral leapt upon him like a furious panther and drove his knife deep into the man's upper chest, just below the collarbone. The Ranger bellowed in pain, and his sword clattered to the cobbled street. The third Ranger rushed toward them, but Kral let his sword fall and tugged the wounded Ranger around. He used the man as a shield, to keep the other two from attacking. The wounded one tried to grab Kral's arms, but the Pict twisted his knife. Agony weakened the Ranger's knees.

Kral shoved the injured Ranger into his comrades. The three of them collided in a tangle of limbs, slipping on the blood-slicked street. Covered by their confusion, Kral broke into a sprint.

Behind him, he heard the thunder of booted feet on pavement and the sounds of voices shouting Aquilonian words he couldn't understand. He raced down the nearest street, turning left at the first corner he came to. It was a narrow alley that curved around, with the far end out of sight. Kral hoped it was not another blind alley. As he rounded the bend, he saw that the other side did open onto a street—this one busier by far than most he'd seen that night.

He drew up short and clung to the shadowed wall. A nearly naked Pict, dark of hair and bronze of skin, bursting into such a crowd, would almost certainly create a commotion. Since his goal was just the opposite—to hide, to slip away unseen—he was hesitant to show himself.

On the other hand, the soldiers and Rangers he had eluded couldn't be far behind. What difference would a few raised eyebrows make if he were to be gutted like a fish either way?

After another moment's consideration, he decided to try to make a bad situation into an advantage. He hurled himself out of the dark alley into the midst of the crowd in the street. A few surprised shouts met his sudden appearance, growing in number and volume as he twisted and wound through the throng. Kral grabbed at women's arms and swatted men on their rears, laughing crazily the whole time.

By the time his pursuers reached the street, it was in chaos. Nobody seemed to know if Kral was a threat or a clown, but the normal patterns of traffic had been disrupted. When a clutch of armed warriors appeared from an alleyway, the crowd's response was near panic. People who had been good-naturedly accepting of Kral's antics realized that something more serious was going on. Everyone tried to see where the Pict had gone.

Kral had almost broken through to a quieter street on the far side of the road when the alarm went up. He had a final, small clutch of people to avoid. When the soldiers started shouting to the people in the street, one of the group pointed at Kral, who was just about to duck around them. Another one reacted quickly enough to shove a walking stick between Kral's legs as he ran.

Kral's trailing leg hit the stick, and the force of it was just enough to trip him, sending him flying into the corner of the stone building at the intersection. He bounced off the wall, bloodied and dazed. He staggered a few more steps down the road, then one of the soldiers was upon him. He slammed Kral to the ground and hurled himself on top of him. His armor pressed down on Kral like a boulder's weight. But Kral reached around behind him with his knife, desperately poking and prodding, looking for a weak spot.

He found it where the top of the man's armor stopped and the neckguard of his helmet was tipped away by the angle at which he lay atop Kral. He

jammed the point of his knife there, found soft, yield-
ing flesh. The man stiffened and rolled away, bellow-
ing with pain. Kral lurched after him, grabbing the
man's helmeted head in a powerful grip. He wrenched
until he heard bones crack. Violent circumstance had
made Kral a killer, and though he took no pleasure in
it, he would do whatever was necessary to preserve
his freedom and continue his quest.

By the time he rose again, the rest of the soldiers
and the Rangers had reached him. A soldier's booted
foot drove into his temple. Bright flashes filled his
eyes, and he went sprawling in the street a third time.
When his vision cleared, he was surrounded, the
points of weapons like a forest of blades directed toward him.

He knew resistance at that point would only get
him killed. Kral preferred to live. To fight another day.

"Stand up, savage," one of the men growled.

Kral shot the speaker an angry glance. It was one of
the Aquilonian soldiers, a slight man with a lean face
and a sharp beak of a nose. His eyes glimmered with
rage as he glared at Kral. The Pict was sure he had
never seen the man before tonight, never done anything to hurt him or his loved ones. And yet, the man
looked as if he'd be happier splitting Kral down the
middle than looking at him for another second. A couple of the other soldiers tended to the body of their
slain comrade.

"What's he done?" another soldier asked.

"Killed our employer, it seems," one of the un-
wounded Rangers said. Kral found that he could understand most of what they said when they spoke in
ordinary terms. His lessons with Alanya had borne
fruit.

"I would not be surprised," the soldier replied. "This
one is no stranger to killing, is he? Did anyone witness
the crime?"

"None that I know," the Ranger said bitterly. "But
this one, and two others, were there. They ran when
they saw us. Our employer, and a fellow Ranger, were
both dead."

"Well, we'll lock him up and sort it out," the soldier said.

"You could simply turn him loose in our care," the
injured Ranger said. Blood had splashed down the
front of his tunic, and he held his hand over his wound,
pressing a strip of cloth to it.

"Maybe we could have before," the soldier said.
"But he's killed one of our own now. And since half
the people in the city have seen him, we prefer to do it
the right way. We will turn him over to the city guard.
If you want to petition them to release him, have at it."

The Rangers grumbled some but finally relented.
No one asked Kral what his preference would be;
but then, he hadn't expected them to. Two soldiers
grabbed his arms and roughly hoisted him to his feet.
The Ranger he had stabbed walked up to him as if
to run him through. A couple of soldiers moved to

intercede, and the Ranger settled for a glancing blow to Kral's cheek with his left fist. Kral tasted blood, then he was yanked away from the Rangers and down the dark, quiet road.

ALANYA WALKED, SLOWLY and sadly, the last few blocks to Cheveray's house. She wanted to let her breathing and heart rate return to something approaching normal. She had avoided her pursuers, but she hadn't seen any sign of Donial or Kral. She guessed that both would find their way back as well. Of Donial, she had no doubt. He knew the city as well as anyone, and he was quick enough to evade pursuit. She worried more about her Pictish friend, Kral, who was not only a stranger in Tarantia, but seemed a bit overwhelmed by the city's size. So far, his survival skills had seemed unparalleled, however, so she still held on to hope.

When she reached Cheveray's street, she saw her brother silhouetted against the glow of a lantern mounted on their friend's gate. She rushed to him and wrapped him in a hug that he accepted grudgingly. "I'm so glad to see you, Donial," she said.

"Any sign of Kral?" he asked, his big dark eyes blinking in the lantern's light. His thick shock of black hair was tousled from the run, his pale cheeks red with effort. He looked younger than his fourteen years at that moment. She guessed she didn't look much better, and ran fingers through her long blond hair. A single year older than he but, with both their parents dead, she was all he had. Her responsibility.

"I haven't seen him. Maybe he's inside already."

"He could never have beaten me here," Donial pointed out. Alanya knew he was right. Even if Donial had taken a more roundabout route back, he was a faster runner than Kral. And he had known where he was going. She felt a sharp pain tug at her. What if something had happened to Kral? After all he had done for her, had she inadvertently delivered him into disaster?

Together, they went quietly into Cheveray's house, which was dark at that hour. Alanya sat in the older man's front room, but Donial seemed full of nervous energy. He paced the floor, sat for a few seconds, then jumped up and paced some more.

After a short while, Cheveray himself appeared, bearing a candle in the hand that didn't hold his cane. He wore white nightclothes and cap, and, with his silver hair and hunched-over posture he looked like some kind of crooked ghost. "Well, children," he said as he entered the room. "What news? Where is your Pictish friend?"

"We don't know, Cheveray," Alanya said gloomily. "He hasn't returned yet. I don't know if he's lost in the city, or captured, or what."

"Captured?" Cheveray echoed. "You were seen, then?"

"Aye," Donial replied. "My fault. I sneezed, just as we were leaving. Dust in the air, or something, I guess, but I couldn't contain it."

"Rangers gave chase," Alanya said, taking up the narrative. "Uncle Lupinius is dead. Slain by unknown murderers, though he yet lived when we arrived. But only for a few moments. Long enough to tell us that the Pictish crown Kral seeks has been stolen. We were leaving Father's house—our house, then, having found my mirror. The house, by all rights, should be mine, and we determined to come back here and talk to you about how to stake my claim. But as Donial said, on our way out we were seen. We split up, to confound our pursuers. Donial and I made our way back here, but we have seen no sign of Kral since."

"I am sorry about your uncle," Cheveray said. "In spite of everything that has happened, he was family, after all."

"I know," Donial said. His expression was sad, his voice subdued in spite of his apparent agitation. "I feel like I should hate him. But seeing him there, injured. Dying. It was awful."

"It always is," Cheveray told them. "Death. We all strive to avoid it, yet finally we greet it, happily or not. I am sure you both were sickened to see your uncle that way, and you unable to help him."

"We tried," Alanya put in. "But we were too late."

"I am certain you did what you could. A most

unfortunate situation. As for your friend, he may yet show up." His warm smile never failed to make Alanya feel better. It did so now as well, in spite of the emotionally wearing night. "It has not been that long, and he is, after all, a stranger here. But he's also a resourceful fellow, unless I have completely lost the knack of judging character."

"He is that," Alanya agreed.

"Then give him a bit more time before you worry," Cheveray said. He put a calming hand on Alanya's shoulder, and she pressed it down with her own. "If he is not here by morning, I'll make some discreet inquiries. Worry not, we shall find him."

Alanya, as always, took comfort from Cheveray's steadiness and uncompromising common sense. She still feared for Kral, but she would wait to panic. Maybe, as Cheveray suggested, everything would be put right by morning.

Or as much as could be done, at any rate. Nothing would bring back her father.

Or her uncle.

2

MORNING CAME, WITH no sign of Kral.

Alanya could hardly eat any of the food that Cheveray's cook put before her. She managed to drink some sweet cider, but her stomach felt like she had swallowed a lead weight.

Kral was missing. Her uncle was dead. It would be impossible to prove that Lupinius was responsible for her father's death.

And Cheveray's cook, an elderly gentleman named Paelin, had mentioned as he served breakfast a rumor he had heard: that King Conan was planning to send a large force out to the borderlands to crush the Pictish rebellion growing there.

Alanya knew there was no growing rebellion. There had simply been Kral, one of the last remnants

of the Bear Clan, searching for the Pictish crown that
her own uncle had stolen from Kral's people during
the attack on their village. Kral had raided Koronaka,
sabotaging the construction of a border wall and trying to get information about the crown. He had become known as the "Ghost of the Wall," since he was
never seen by anyone who lived to tell of it. If the rumor of an Aquilonian response was true, it just meant
that tales of Kral's activities had made their way back
to the King.

In Kral's absence the clan's only surviving woman
had taken his place, so even though he was here in
Aquilonia, the activities of the "Ghost" continued.
Settlers and soldiers had already killed the rest of
their village, save one old man.

Surely Conan wouldn't believe those exaggerated
stories. The King had, after all, sent Alanya's father,
Invictus, to the borderlands to expand upon the peace
that had been established between Koronaka and the
Picts of the Bear Clan. It had been Uncle Lupinius,
not the Picts, who had broken that peace, using
Alanya's burgeoning relationship with Kral as an excuse. The settlers had slaughtered the clan, murdering
her father along with it. Possibly Conan would send
soldiers to exact revenge for her father's death—but
the total destruction of the Bear Clan village would
seem to be payment enough.

Donial, she knew, still slept. She hadn't seen Cheveray this morning, but as she sat alone at the breakfast

table, trying not to look at the uneaten meal, he came in from outside.

"I have put some inquiries into motion," he told Alanya. "If Kral has been arrested or detained by any authorities, civil or military, we'll find out about it soon enough. Further, I've started some of my associates researching the details of your father's estate. We shall have you set up in that house in no time."

"Thank you, Cheveray," Alanya said. She was sure she didn't sound very heartened, however.

"What's wrong?"

"All that," Alanya said. "And more." She told Cheveray about the rumor she had heard from Paelin. "There is no Pictish invasion," she insisted. "That's just stories blown out of proportion."

"Well, then, if King Conan does send an army, that is what they shall discover," Cheveray suggested.

"Perhaps," Alanya said. "But maybe they'll decide that as long as they have traveled so far, they might as well go ahead and kill the rest of the Picts."

"Never had much use for them myself," Cheveray said. "But your friend Kral seems decent enough."

"He's wonderful!" Alanya retorted. "If not for him, I would not be here now. I would still be trapped in Koronaka. Or more likely, dead on the road between there and here."

"Then we all owe him a debt that can never be repaid, Alanya," Cheveray said, with obvious sincerity. "For you are truly a special young lady, and one without whom the world would indeed be a far grimmer place."

Alanya smiled in spite of herself. "Can you talk to the King, then?" she pleaded, the quick grin already fading. "If there is war between Aquilonia and the Picts, then all my father's work, and his death, will have been in vain."

Cheveray looked serious when he answered. "I will try," he promised. "But I can make no guarantees. If these events have already been set in motion, it will be most difficult to bring them to a sudden halt. The course of history flows only one way, child, never forget that. That is why it's easier not to make a mistake in the first place than to take it back once it has been made."

Alanya swallowed and nodded. It had, she supposed, been her bad judgment, leaving Koronaka by herself to go off into the woods, that had started this entire chain of events. That's where she had met Kral, and they had become friends. And where they had been observed by Donial. Uncle Lupinius had used that as an excuse to raid the Pictish village, killing everyone they found. Things had escalated from there, with the result that her father and uncle were dead, and so was virtually everyone Kral had ever known.

The only consolation—and it was scant indeed—was that she was home, back in Tarantia, and that her father's residence, the house in which she had grown up, would soon be hers. She and Donial would live there together, with whatever fragments of their father's staff they could persuade to stay on. Kral could have a place there, too, if he wanted. She suspected that he would not make that decision. Once he managed to reclaim the Teeth of the Ice Bear crown, which Lupinius had stolen from his clan, he would return it to its proper place in the Pictish wilderness and stay there to rebuild. Kral cared little for cities or civilization. It was obvious from his every word and gesture since he'd been in Tarantia that the place was far too large and crowded for his liking. He was a true child of the wilderness and would never be happy, Alanya believed, unless he was surrounded by trees and rivers and the creatures that dwelled there.

They were what they were—she a city girl, born and bred in Aquilonia's heart, and he a barbarian from the dark forests of the far west. If she could find him again—*when* she found him, mentally correcting herself, determined to remain optimistic—she would just have to enjoy his company for as long as they were together. The gulf between them was too wide to be spanned forever. Ultimately, they would stand on its opposite sides.

She took another sip of cider, nibbled halfheartedly on a biscuit, and wondered where he might be.

•   •   •

TREMONT'S FINGERS WERE nearly as long and thin as the dagger he wielded. He was a thief, who the night before had posed as a wealthy nobleman named Declariat. Thus he found himself in possession of that which he had stolen: a worthless-looking, barbaric crown made of bones and teeth. He had acquired it at the behest of one Bresson, to whom he often sold stolen goods. But once Bresson saw what he had sent Tremont after, he wanted no part of the thing. Which meant that Tremont had murdered two people and put himself in considerable jeopardy for nothing.

Well, he was not willing to let it be for nothing. The teeth with which the crown was embedded were unusual, for their size if nothing else. It was his intention to pry them loose and sell them as curios. That would net a few coins, at least. Then he could sell the bone framework to someone else. Someone like the very man he had pretended to be, who did indeed have a reputation as someone who collected examples of barbaric handiwork. Since the man had never seen the crown with the teeth in place, he would likely pay just as much for it without them as he would have with them. That way, Tremont could pocket a little extra for the odd, huge teeth. And if Declariat wouldn't pay for the crown, someone else would.

Tremont didn't stand to make a lot for his night's work. He seldom did. He got by, stealing a little here and a little there. His apartment was small and crowded. Most nights, someone with even less luck than he slept on his doorstep. The building was far from peaceful, with the sounds of fighting and love-making and the constant battle against vermin always filling the air. Tremont was lean by nature, but that trait was made more pronounced by the fact that some-times entire days would go by without a meal. Other days, his meals would consist of whatever scraps of food he could scrounge. Bresson had tried to help, by steering him to the crown, and now Tremont was de-termined to realize something for his troubles.

Tremont's stomach growled as he poked at the teeth, trying to work them loose from the fine copper wire that held them in place. He would feast tonight.

One way or another.

THE CELL IN which Kral found himself was dank and dark and smelled horrible. It was just wide enough for him to lie down in, but if he stretched his arms over his head, he could touch both sides of it at once. Not that he wanted to lie down on the floor. He had a feeling it had been a very long time since it had been washed.

In the wilderness, the ground was constantly re-plenished. Wind and rain scoured the earth. But here, in the tiny cage deep underground, the elements never reached. Kral wanted to pace, but with only a couple of steps he was as far as he could go. He felt as if he would explode if he had to stay there for very long. Being caged was the worst thing that could happen to a Pict—far better to have died in battle, painted and screaming for the heads of his enemies.

He had been taken to the city guardsmen by the Aquilonian soldiers. They had peppered him with questions about Lupinius's murder, to which he had replied with a version of the truth. He had sought an object stolen from his people. The Ranger had been dead when he arrived, and Lupinius murdered. He had called for help, to which the Rangers on hand at the estate could attest. Lupinius had died before anyone had arrived. All he left out was the presence of Alanya and Donial. When the guardsmen told him the Rangers had insisted they chased three, not one, Kral simply held firm, saying they were mistaken. After all, if they chased three, where were the other two? Were they saying he was the easiest to catch?

Later that night, two guardsmen bearing torches had led him down a winding staircase and past a series of barred doors to his cell. Behind some of those doors he heard snoring or bizarre mutterings, and he wondered how long some of these people had been here.

He believed it was morning, but there was no real way to tell. No light from the sun reached the cell. He could hear more of his fellow prisoners moving about than he had during the night, and he was sure several

hours had passed, during which he had slept only fit-
fully on the straw ticking provided.

He sat on the straw, knees bent, forearms resting
on them. He would wither away and die there. And
since he had killed an Aquilonian soldier, he had little doubt that he was fated to do exactly that.

Unless they took him out and put him to death
first.

Kral felt hopelessness descend on him like night
over the forest. He had failed to find the Teeth and return it to its home in the Ice Bear's cave. What the result of his failure would be, he didn't know. He could
only speculate that it would be disastrous for the Pictish people, or the crown would not have been so
carefully tended for all these generations.

He would probably never again know the forests
and fields and mountains of his homeland, never again
feel the freedom of running between the trees, with no
company but birds and sky. He tried to hold out hope
that Alanya would somehow find him here and rescue
him. But he knew, deep down, how unlikely that was.
Even if she did discover his whereabouts, how could
she free him? She was no warrior, to break into a
prison and liberate its inmates. Neither was Donial, or
Cheveray for that matter. And they were Aquilonian,
after all, so breaking their own laws to get him out
would not be something they would do lightly.

No, he had to stay alert for any possible chance to

get himself out of here. But failing that, he had to allow for the likelihood that these dark walls and barred door would be the last things he would ever see.

"You in there," he heard a voice say. Older, male, raspy. "I can tell by your breathing that you're awake. Tell me, what of the world outside? Is the Cimmerian still king, or has the Aquilonian nobility risen up to depose the barbarian?"

"If you speak to me," Kral answered, "and you refer to Conan, then yes, he still reigns. I saw him myself. It was only last night, though it seems a year or more."

"You are no Hyborian," the voice said.

"I am Kral, a Pict."

"A Pict?" Surprise was evident in the aged one's voice. "Yet you speak our tongue."

"I said I am a Pict, not that I am stupid," Kral protested. "Yes, I speak your tongue."

"Your accent is terrible," the man said. "But I can understand you. How do you come to be in here?"

"I was being chased by some Aquilonian soldiers— over a misunderstanding—and defending myself, killed one of them."

"They do not take that lightly around here," the man said.

Kral had not expected that they would. "How long have you been in here?"

The man hesitated before answering. "Honestly, I know not," he said. "Conan had not yet taken the throne when I was arrested. I remember that much. I killed, as well—two men, in fact, who had cheated me in a game of chance. Or I believed they had. I was more than a little drunk, so I am not altogether sure."

"So . . . you have been here for years," Kral said. "And they have not executed you for your crimes but just left you to rot?"

The man chuckled, a wet, unpleasant sound. "That about sums it up," he said. "Often, I suspect they have forgotten I yet exist."

"I never forget you're here, Totlio," another voice called.

"That's Carillus, our jailer," the old man called Totlio explained. "Carillus, be kind to our young friend here. He is not from these parts."

"I could tell by the accent," Carillus said. Kral couldn't see him from where he sat, and preferred not to get up and go to the door just now. Carillus sounded much younger than Totlio, and healthier. "Where are you from, dog?"

"He's a Pict," Totlio answered before Kral could.

"A Pict? Good Aquilonian, then, for a savage."

Totlio chuckled again, and it turned into a rasping cough. "Don't get him started," he said when he was able. "He'll tell you that savages can learn languages just as well as any of us."

"We can," Kral declared. "I can speak your tongue, yet I have not heard either of you speaking Pictish."

Carillus joined in Totlio's laughter. "You make a

good point," he said. "I think I will enjoy having you around, young Pict. Maybe we will get to keep you for a while."

Kral couldn't think of anything that would be worse.

3

A DAY HAD passed, then another. Lupinius's body was on display at the house, prior to its cremation. Alanya and Donial had agreed with Cheveray's suggestion that they not visit the body or the house during that time. Alanya's feelings about it were mixed, confused. He had been family, as much as she had hated him at times. Her last surviving family, besides her brother. But she still believed he had killed her father. Cheveray had speculated that if Lupinius's Rangers, who knew them both, saw them in Tarantia, they might be held as accomplices in their uncle's murder. Chances were they had captured Kral and already guessed that Alanya and Donial were responsible for his presence in the city.

There had been no word of Kral. Cheveray insisted that his people, whoever they might be, were working on reclaiming Alanya and Donial's house for them and working on finding out what had become of Kral.

Alanya just lounged in Cheveray's house all day, mourning and moping. Donial tried to stay close by, in case she needed him. But he had taken the opportunity to go visit a few close friends in the city. At Alanya's insistence, he had sworn them to secrecy. She didn't want people to know they were back in Tarantia until they had settled the matter of their father's estate. She said that if others were planning to lay claim to the place, it would be better if their presence here was a surprise, just in case. Donial suspected that embarrassment was part of it. Alanya just didn't want her friends to know her unsettled state. She was still despondent over their father's death, Kral's disappearance, and the uncertainty over their house.

He had been talking things over with friends this morning, though. When he found Alanya in the room she used at Cheveray's house, he had a suggestion.

"We need a champion," he announced eagerly.

"A champion?" Her blue eyes were only half-open, and Donial suspected he had awakened her when he charged in. "For what?"

"We are making no progress, Cheveray's way," he said. "He's a wonderful man, but his methods are slow. Bureaucratic. We need a man of action. Someone who will take our side and battle on our behalf to win the fights we cannot win ourselves. Someone like Conan, who has never been bested in combat."

"Is that really true?" Alanya asked.

"If he has been, I have never heard of it," Donial hedged.

"Do you know of anyone else like that?" Alanya pressed. "It seems anyone with a distinguished record like that would be well-known. Why would such a warrior choose to be our champion?"

"I was talking to Tan and Ellin, and they both had heard of a Cimmerian who is in Tarantia. A huge mountain of a man, they say. Good with a sword and quick with his fists. You know how seldom Cimmerians emerge from their own land. But this one, according to them, wanted to see a civilized place where a Cimmerian could be king. Now he finds himself stuck here with little money and few friends. Tan says he might be open to an offer of gainful employment."

"And how does Tan know all this?" Alanya asked him. Her eyes were wider now, with their usually bright sparkle.

"His father is at home with a broken arm and a shattered jaw," Donial explained. "From having encountered this Cimmerian in a tavern, three nights back."

"You think this Cimmerian can be found in that same tavern tonight?" Alanya wondered.

"It's worth a try," Donial said. "What do we have to lose?"

• • •

ALANYA WAS HESITANT to go inside the Pig and
Barley Tavern. From the outside, it sounded like a
rowdy place, full of men boozing and brawling. If
there were any women at all in there, they probably
weren't the kind she had ever been acquainted with.
She could hear raucous laughter and booming voices.

But she wasn't letting Donial enter alone, that much
was certain. At fourteen, he was not old enough to get
himself out of trouble in a place like that and just
young enough to get into it. She would stay close beside him, believing that her additional year gave her
an edge.

"Are we going in?" Donial asked urgently. He
looked as grown-up as a boy with a baby face and
long, dark curls could. He wore a simple blue tunic,
belted at the waist, with a long dirk suspended from a
gold chain. Tight breeches and leather sandals completed his outfit. Alanya had worn a shift that covered
most of her but was loose enough to let her run if
need be.

"Yes," she said. "Let's go."

Donial flashed her a wicked smile and pushed
through the door. The noise inside seemed to increase
almost unbearably, and Alanya followed her brother
in, as if forcing her way through a solid wall of sound.

Inside, a few lamps burned, casting illumination

into the main chamber but leaving the corners awash in shadow. The place stank of ale and sweat and lamp oil. She had been correct; the tavern was mostly full of men, with a few barely dressed women plying questionable trades off in the shadowed areas. Many of the men were big and muscular, but even in that company, there was no mistaking which one was the Cimmerian.

He sat alone at a table near the center of the tavern. Lined up in front of him were a dozen empty tankards, and there was another mug in his giant fist. His hair was as black as night, crudely cut as if with a dull knife. His eyes were as gray as Alanya believed the skies of his distant homeland must be. He wore a shirt of some rough fabric, with a leather sword belt at his waist and a tanned leather skirt below that. Sandals were strapped up his ankles. On the table, crowded by his empties, were a broadsword and a dented helmet. His neck was massive, as big around as Alanya's thigh, or bigger. She wasn't sure she had ever seen arms so corded with steely sinew. He wasn't striking, as Conan had been, but there was a definite sense of strength and power about him. Maybe, Alanya thought, Donial was right. The man looked as if he could accomplish just about anything.

Donial reached him first. "Is your name Conor, of Cimmeria?" he asked.

The barbarian's head turned from side to side as if he were searching for something. After a moment, he lowered his gaze and rested it on Donial. "It might be," he said in accented Aquilonian. "Does he owe you any money?"

"I have never met him before," Donial replied, "else I would not be asking you if you are he."

The big man drained his tankard and slammed the empty down on the table. "Another, barkeep!" he shouted. Then he looked at Donial again. "What you say makes sense, boy."

It was obvious now that he had emptied all those tankards himself. He swayed a little bit as he regarded Donial, then his eyes widened as he noticed Alanya standing behind him. "Is you with her?" he asked. "I mean, is she with you?"

"I am with him," Alanya said. She had intended to be discreet, but almost had to shout just to make herself heard over the general din. "I am his sister. If you are indeed Conor, as we believe, we would like to hire you to do a job for us."

Conor started to lift a tankard to his mouth but realized his hand was empty and pressed his palm flat against the table instead. "What kind of a job?"

"More than one, actually," Donial answered. "We need someone to help us take back our father's house, which others have moved into. Also, we have a friend who's missing. We need him found and returned to us, wherever he might be. And finally, there is an object that's been stolen from him, which we need found and brought back to us."

"Would there be fighting involved in this?" the barbarian asked eagerly. "Killing, maybe?"

"There could be," Alanya said.

"And you will pay me?"

"In gold," Donial replied.

Conor smiled. "Then I am your man."

"We thought as much," Alanya said.

"But not tonight."

"Not tonight?" Alanya echoed.

"I am much too busy tonight," Conor explained.

He didn't look terribly busy to Alanya. "Busy doing what?"

Conor eyed her as if she were insane. "Drinking." He looked again at his hand, apparently surprised that it remained empty. "Barkeep!" he shouted.

The overwrought barkeep rushed another tankard into his outstretched hand.

"And I think I'll get into a fight later," Conor added.

"Well, then," Alanya said, "it's easy to see why you cannot start anything new tonight."

"Exactly!" the Cimmerian shouted. "I am glad you understand." He squinted his eyes and stared at Alanya. "Do you know that back in Taern I am not only considered the best fighter, but also the best lover? Women wait for weeks for a turn with me, and men keep their distance lest I decide to knock them around just to see them fall."

"How wonderful for you," Alanya said. "I am surprised you ever left."

"Wanted to see where Conan got to," Conor said. "He's the King here, you know."

"So I have heard," Alanya said. Donial just stood to the side now, watching his sister through eyes wide with amazement. "Conor, we need help, and we are willing to pay for it. If this interests you, tomorrow when you have sobered up you can come and talk to us." She told him where Cheveray's house was. "If you can find it, you have the job."

She turned on her heel and stalked away. Donial followed. When they were outside and not surrounded by that infernal racket, she heard Donial laughing. "What?" she demanded.

"The way you talked to him. He could have torn your head off with his little finger."

"He would have had to figure out which of my three heads to go after," she said. "I'm sure he saw at least that many."

"Do you think he will find us tomorrow?"

"I know not how much he will remember about tonight," Alanya said. "Hard to say if he will know how to find us, even if he does have some vague memory that we spoke."

"Maybe we should have written the address down."

"You believe he can read?" Alanya asked. "You give him far more credit than I."

Donial considered for a moment. "No, I suppose

not, though someone might have read it to him. I hope he can find us, though."

"As do I, Donial," Alanya said at last. "Mitra knows we need some kind of help."

GORIAN HAD NEVER shied away from violence. It could be a useful tool sometimes, and when his master required that it be committed, he was happy to do so.

Tonight, apparently, it was required.

On the orders of Kanilla Rey, who had magically traced the barbaric crown that Gorian and his comrades had failed to find a few nights earlier, he had taken a different crew of men to the shabby apartment of a skinny, not terribly successful thief named Tremont. The place smelled like spoiled meat.

In this case, Tremont had been at least partially successful. He still had the crown. Or most of it, at any rate. It sat on a small, rough-hewn table in Tremont's pit of an apartment.

Not all of it, though. He had taken some of the big teeth out of it, and had already sold them. Which was a problem for Kanilla Rey, who wanted the whole thing. Complete and intact.

And Tremont would not, or could not, tell Gorian to whom he had sold the missing teeth.

Hence the violence. A short but absurdly muscular

Shemite held Tremont's arms behind his back. Two more helpers, both Aquilonians, stood by waiting their turns at the thief. As usual, Gorian had met none of them before.

Gorian tilted the thief's chin toward him, eyed the blood that ran in a line from his mouth. "Tremont," he said gently, "are you sure you don't remember yet?"

Tremont dazedly shook his head. "He was a man on a street. I showed him the teeth. He bought a couple."

Gorian had heard this same sentence, or a variation on it, several times in the past few minutes. He drew his fist back, held it a minute, taking careful aim, and then drove it hard into the man's flat stomach. Tremont bent over under the blow. It was all the Shemite could do to hold him upright. Tremont's long, fine hair, wet with sweat, swung as his head flew forward and then back.

"What man?" Gorian demanded. "What street?"

Tremont breathed through his mouth for a moment before answering. "I remember not."

The sad part was, Gorian had begun to believe he was telling the truth.

But he had to be sure. He wasn't yet. Not completely. He didn't think Tremont could stand up to this sort of battering for very long, but maybe a little while longer.

He was about to strike again when the door to Tremont's apartment swung open behind him. He turned to look, and what he saw made his blood run cold.

Three Stygians in black robes, their hems dragging along the floor, stood in the doorway. They were slight men, dusky-skinned, and holding no weapons.

But Gorian had never felt such menace in his life.

4

ONE OF THE Stygians extended a bony hand. "We will have the crown," he said. His voice was as creaky as an old mast in a windstorm.

A sword scraped from its scabbard, and Gorian saw that one of his Aquilonian allies held it. "You can just turn around and go back where you came from," the man said. "The crown is ours."

The Stygian who had spoken barely glanced at the swordsman. He waved his right hand, wiggling his fingers as he did, almost as if dismissing a useless servant.

The Aquilonian—a burly man, at least twice the scrawny Stygian's weight—dropped to the ground instantly. His muscles might as well have turned to liquid beneath his skin.

Gorian's blood ran cold. The Stygian hadn't touched the man, merely gestured toward him. At the same time, he knew that if he let the crown get away from him again, Kanilla Rey would not be any more forgiving.

Instead of confronting the Stygians, he jerked a thumb toward the battered and bleeding Tremont. "He has it."

The Stygian turned to Tremont, who regarded him from bruised, swollen eyes. "We will have the crown," the man said again.

"You might as well take it," Tremont managed to utter. "You or them, it doesn't matter to me."

The Shemite released him and locked eyes with Gorian. Gorian knew the big man wanted to fight the Stygians for the prize. He had more faith in his strength than Gorian did. Gorian recognized that whatever magic the Stygians possessed was more powerful than any normal man, and quite possibly stronger than Kanilla Rey's as well.

Slowly, breaking eye contact with the Shemite but keeping the Stygians in his sights, he backed away from them. If it came to more trouble, he wanted a solid wall at his back, and nothing else.

Suddenly, it was clear that more trouble was on the way. The Shemite lunged for the crown, scooping it off the table. Ducking his head, he tried to charge right through the Stygians blocking the doorway.

There was no contest. One of the Stygians waved

his hand and whispered a phrase that Gorian couldn't hear. The Shemite stopped short, as if he had run into an impenetrable barrier. He staggered back a couple of steps, and his fingers relaxed. The crown slipped from them.

With one powerful exhalation, the Shemite slumped to the floor, obviously dead.

But the crown hovered in the air a moment—long enough for the nearest of the Stygians to grab it.

Gorian knew that resistance would only get him killed. Intent on surviving the encounter, he pretended to faint. He let his eyes swivel up in his skull and fell against the wall, then slid to the floor.

With his eyes closed, he heard the rasp of fabric, the soft murmur of hushed voices speaking in a tongue he didn't understand. Then nothing. Minutes passed. Finally, he dared to open his eyes a slit.

Two bodies lay on the ground where he expected them to be. The other Aquilonian still stood where he had been, petrified with fear. His eyes were wide and liquid. Tremont had sagged to the floor, visibly trembling like a leaf in a high wind.

The Stygians were gone.

With the crown that Kanilla Rey wanted.

"We will have to tell him we failed," Gorian said quietly. "He won't be happy."

It took a minute, but eventually the Aquilonian managed to turn his head and look at Gorian. He didn't speak, just slowly nodded his understanding.

Gorian didn't look forward to that part, not at all.

But even if Kanilla Rey chose to kill him, at least the deed would not be done by strangers, in that foul-smelling place.

He could take some comfort in that. Maybe not much, but after such an encounter, even a little would do.

CONOR MANAGED TO find Cheveray's house the next day, much to Alanya's surprise. His skin was ashen, his eyes bloodshot and bleary. She had heard that Cimmerians could hold their liquor, but this one definitely seemed to be suffering the consequences of his consumption the night before.

"You," he said when she opened the door at his knock. "You are the girl . . . from last night."

"Yes," Alanya confirmed. "I am. Have you thought about our offer?"

"Thought about it," Conor said. "I cannot exactly remember all of it. There were many parts, as I recall. But I remembered how to find you."

"You did, at that. Come in." She backed away from the door and let the big man enter. "Let me fetch my brother."

She left Conor standing in Cheveray's front room while she dashed to get Donial. They had argued, on the way back from the tavern the night before, about how they would actually pay Conor if he did accept their offer. Neither had any source of income, or much of value beyond her mirror.

"We will just have to make it clear to him that he needs to be successful," Donial had insisted. "If we get Father's house restored to us, there is a certain amount of wealth that comes with it, right?"

"We think so," Alanya said. "But we do not know that for sure."

"Well, if we're wrong, then he can have some of the more valuable items there, and he can sell them himself," Donial suggested. "That seems fair."

Alanya had been willing to grant the point last night. Now, in the light of day, with a gigantic armed barbarian standing by the front door, she wasn't so sure.

It was a little late to change course, though. She burst through the door of Donial's room and found him dozing. "Donial!" she said, shaking him awake. "He's here!"

"Who?" Donial mumbled.

"The Cimmerian, from last night. Conor. He waits in the front room, to talk to us about our offer."

Donial's eyes snapped wide open. "Conor is here?"

He was alert instantly, and together they returned to find the big man standing right where Alanya had left him, staring into space.

"Conor?" Alanya said.

He focused on them, stifling a yawn. He had not bathed since the night before, and the stink of dried sweat mixed with alcohol came off him in waves. "Yes, I remember you, too," he said, nodding toward Donial. "Must not have had as much fun as I thought."

"I see no new bruises," Donial said. "Maybe you failed to find that fight after all."

"Oh, I fought," Conor said. "Like a tiger. Why, back home in Taern, I—"

"You told us all about that," Alanya reminded him. "May we get to business."

"Right," Conor agreed. "What is it you need done, again?"

Alanya took the lead. "There has been an object stolen from a friend of ours. We want it found. Also, our friend is missing, and we need him found. We are working on that one, already. Last, our father died and others moved into his house before we could. It rightfully belongs to us. We are working on that one, too, but if it comes to a fight, we would like you on our side."

"Fighting I can do," Conor said with a grin, as if remembering happy days back in Taern. "Finding things is harder."

"How about finding a thief?"

"Probably," Conor admitted.

They haggled for a few minutes over a price, finally agreeing on one that Alanya felt comfortable they could pay—if they recovered their father's estate. If they didn't, they would have to borrow from Cheveray.

Once they had settled that, Alanya and Donial described the crown to Conor as best they could, neither of them having ever laid eyes on it. They told him when it had been stolen, and from where. Alanya knew that if they never found Kral, it would do them no good to have located the crown. But she still held out hope that he would turn up. When he did, she wanted to be able to hand over the crown so that he would not insist on going after it.

If she failed, and Kral went looking for the thing, she would go along for the hunt. She owed him that much. But she really didn't want to have to leave Tarantia behind again. Better to have their hired champion locate it and bring it back before that became an issue.

Armed with the description and a couple of coins as a kind of advance payment, Conor left to get to work. He seemed particularly happy with the idea that he might have to knock some heads together in the Thieves' Quarter to find what he sought.

"I AM NOT sure how long I can stand this." Kral was not someone prone to complaining, but he felt his muscles stiffening already, shrinking from lack of use, from sitting in the Aquilonian prison cell. "How do you do it?" he asked.

"You try not to think about it too much," Totlio suggested. "If you dwell on the days and weeks and months that are passing, you'll go mad. I have seen it happen. Think about other things. I have composed an epic poem in here. Seven hundred and two stanzas, and counting. All in my head."

Kral was astounded by the enormity of such an undertaking. "Surely you cannot remember all of that."

"You would be surprised what you can do with your mind if you've no other use for it," Totlio said from the darkness of the next cell.

"It's either that or annoy me with his constant nattering," the voice of Carillus joined in.

A voice Kral had not heard before sounded. "Annoy all of us, you mean!" Laughter from other, unseen cells greeted this remark.

"You, young Pict, might as well start some project of your own," Carillus suggested. "You will doubtless be here awhile yet."

Kral felt his spirits sink at the man's prediction. He had expected nothing else, but hearing it stated so bluntly still depressed him.

"If you had only killed a Ranger, that would be one thing," the guard continued. "Or even just him and his employer."

"Who I did not kill," Kral protested.

"So you say. But killing one of the King's soldiers? If you ever leave here alive, it will be because you're headed for the chopping block."

That was a chance Kral was almost willing to take.

He could not get out of his cell alone, he had determined. But if he was taken out for virtually any reason, he would have only the strength of humans—not stone walls—to contend with.

He didn't know if he could prevail.

But at least he would have a chance.

IN THE WILDERNESS at the western edge of the continent, the sun shone down on an unusual gathering of Pictish clan leaders. Heaps of human skulls punctuated the meeting place. Smoke from at least two dozen fires hung in a haze over the village of the Elk Clan, where the leaders had agreed to meet, filling the place with the smell of burning wood and charred meat. Chiefs from nine clans had gathered to smoke pipes, eat and drink together, and discuss the looming problem of the Teeth of the Ice Bear's disappearance. More were expected within days.

They sat on stones or downed logs or simply on the dirt in the main campfire area, in front of the clan's Great Hut. Tangled elk antlers stood on either side of the big hut's doorway, in mounds taller than the tallest of the Picts. Usam, the Elk Clan's chief, a wrinkled old man wearing faded buckskins decorated with painted designs and a long spray of feathers, sat in front of his hut on a chair made of antlers with leather stretched between them.

He smiled, looking upon the assemblage before

him. Interclan warfare had always prevented any kind
of long-term unity among the various Pictish clans.
The Aquilonians, constantly pushing westward, had
posed a threat, but that threat had seemed best dealt
with on a clan-by-clan basis. Never had there been
one that menaced all equally.

But everything had changed. The youth, Kral, had
promised to regain the Teeth and return it to its proper
place in the Bear Clan village. Without the Teeth
there, the Ice Bear would once again walk the Earth,
destroying everything he came into contact with. One
sweep across the wilderness could eliminate all the
clans, and the forests that supported them, forever.

But Kral had gone away, leaving only Klea and
Mang in his place. Klea was doing her part to harass
the settlers at Koronaka. She still sought the Teeth.
Mang had devoted himself to traveling from clan to
clan, trying to bring everyone together.

Usam considered himself a visionary and saw the
possibilities others had missed. He offered the Elk
Clan's village as an impartial meeting place. It looked
as if most of the clans would send their chieftains, or
at least an elder, as a representative. Each one who
came brought gifts, of course, as tradition dictated—
Usam had enough meat for the winter already stacked
behind his hut, if it could all be salted and preserved
in time. His women were working on that now.

More important than their gifts, however, was the

simple fact that they were visitors in his village. When they all agreed on unification, as he was certain they would, they would be his guests. They would naturally look to him for leadership.

Leadership he would be happy to provide . . .

5

ALANYA STOOD IN the courtyard of her father's house—her house, now—with Donial by her side. The remaining staff, five of the twelve who had once been employed here, were arranged before them on the stairs leading up to the large front door. They all smiled warmly at the siblings and seemed happy they had returned. For her part, Alanya felt as if she had thrown off an enormous burden. Not that she was happy yet—as long as Kral remained missing, she wouldn't be. But she was closer to it than she had been.

Lupinius's body had finally been removed from the grounds and burned on a pyre. She and Donial had kept away from the final ceremony. Cheveray had, through his contacts, put out the word that the two young people had only just arrived in Tarantia—too late for the funeral, and therefore too late to have had a hand in the murder. He had learned that the surviving Rangers—Calvert, Trey, Constantus, Ondene, and Kelvan—had already sought and found other employment, so the chances that they would be actively looking for Lupinius's killer were slim.

As mistress of the house, she knew she should say something. Her father would have, at any rate. He always seemed to have the right words for any given situation. She thought it over, and finally came up with a few sentences, which she delivered with as much confidence as she could muster.

"Thank you all for staying," she said. As she spoke, she let her gaze roam over the group. They were all, to a man or woman, old. Older, probably, than the parents of her parents. They had probably stayed on because they had no better place to be, nothing else they could do.

The reason didn't matter. The fact that they were here was good enough. "I know my father treated you all well," she continued. "Like family. How Uncle Lupinius treated you I cannot say, but I would guess not the same way."

She paused, in case any of them wanted to respond. But they were silent, just watching her. "Thanks to the efforts of our father's friend Cheveray, the house of Invictus is now the house of Alanya and Donial. You are all welcome to stay on here, in your present capacities, if you so choose. If you prefer not to, we understand that and wish you the best. You will all continue to be paid, and you can stay in your own rooms. Nothing need change except who is mistress of the house."

Alanya wasn't yet sure how she would live up to those promises, just as she didn't know how she would pay Conor, if he earned anything at all. Cheveray had promised her that money would not be a problem, that Invictus had wealth that would become hers. But she didn't know if that was true; hadn't seen any indication of it, anyway. So she was a bit nervous about that part.

"Anyway," she went on, "like I said, we are happy that you are all here. And we are very happy to be home, where we belong. So thank you all."

The servants stood there for a moment longer. Alanya turned to Donial, making it clear that they had been dismissed. "How was that?" she asked.

"Not bad," he said. "Father would have done it better. Or me. But not bad, for you."

Little brothers, she thought. "I should have left you in the woods."

"Was it your choice?" he replied.

She didn't bother to dignify his remark with an answer, but went inside her home—her home!—to savor the sensation.

Cheveray had summoned her from her room earlier that day, announcing that a visitor waited downstairs for her and Donial. Both had hurried down, expecting that it might be Conor with some news about the Teeth.

It was a Cimmerian. But not Conor.

She recognized him as soon as she entered the room. He stood near the window, blocking most of the light that came in. He was a massive figure. He wore a pale blue silk blouse, belted at the waist with a wide leather girdle to which a broadsword and a long dagger were attached. Below that were black breeches of some fine material, tucked into tooled-leather boots. A few streaks of gray showed in his black hair, but not many. When he moved toward her, she could see that his face and arms were scarred from a thousand battles. Blue eyes blazed in that face, but his smile was warm and meant to put her at ease.

She fell to her knees the moment she recognized him, with a furtive glance back to make sure that Donial did the same.

"Your highness," she said. "Cheveray said not who was here, and I did not hear your approach."

"I came in alone," King Conan said. His voice was friendly but firm, with a slight rasp of age. "My retinue waits in the street."

"But . . . why come here?" Donial asked. From the tightness in his words, Alanya could tell that he was nervous. She was, too. She could barely control the shaking in her limbs. She waited anxiously to see if he would answer Donial's question or strike him for being so impudent as to ask it.

"Because Cheveray asked me to," Conan answered. "And because your father was a man I trusted implicitly."

"But—"

"Rise, Alanya. Donial. I am not one to stand on ceremony, particularly in the house of an old friend."

Alanya obeyed at once, though the motion put her at the mercy of her own unstable legs. The King seemed to recognize her distress and pointed to chairs. "Sit, please," he said. "You, too, Cheveray."

The old man lowered himself to a seat with a grateful sigh. Alanya and Donial followed suit.

"Cheveray explains to me that you find yourselves in an awkward situation," Conan said, when he had also taken a chair. "Your uncle Lupinius had laid claim to your father's estate. He said further that the two of you were missing in the Pictish wilderness and presumed dead. Given those circumstances, his claim could hardly be denied. Since the night of his murder, the house, grounds, and all property belonging to your father have been under guard. Had you not come forward, it would have become property of Tarantia."

"But we are not missing, or dead," Donial pointed out.

"Of course not," the King agreed with a grin. "We know that now. Which means that all of Invictus's lands and wealth—including what I suspect you'll find a generous pension—belong to you. I would rather return your father to you, alive and well. Since that is beyond the realm of the possible, I hope that you will accept these things as partial payment. He served me well, and I should like to reward his children, in the absence of being able to reward him."

Alanya was at a loss for words. Could this really be happening? The legendary king of Aquilonia, sitting with her and asking her to accept something from him?

She realized that he was waiting for her to say something, to give a response to his request. His eyes burned into her, and she felt her cheeks crimsoning beneath his gaze. "Yes, your highness, of course we will accept any generosity you choose to offer us."

"It is not generosity," Conan corrected. "Simply your due. I am sure you had a hard time on the border, especially when the truce failed."

"But, your highness," Alanya said, unable to contain herself. "The Pictish threat has been vastly overstated. I know that—"

Conan cut her off. "My intelligence suggests otherwise," he said. "I know not precisely what happened at the Bear Clan village, although I hear that there are conflicting stories. But my agents in the area tell me that something seems to be in the offing now, and I've ordered a force to the region to respond to it."

She wanted to say more, to ask after Kral, to know

a thousand things about the relationship her father had had with him. But he rose and tossed a smile toward Cheveray. "I must be off, old friend. Thank you for bringing this situation to my attention, and I am glad that I was able to help. As for you two—follow in your father's footsteps if you can. Work to keep the peace between Aquilonia and our neighbors. Since you are Invictus's offspring, I'm convinced that if you simply follow your hearts, you will make valuable contributions."

Alanya cast Cheveray an imploring gaze, silently begging him to ask the King to stay longer. He responded with a shake of his head. Barely perceptible, but she understood it. *Leave him alone,* it meant. *Be happy with what you have.*

After the King was gone, she and Donial turned to one another and burst out laughing.

That had been early afternoon. Now she looked around the home that Conan had restored to her. The staff had done their best to clean up, after the ravages of Lupinius and his Rangers. Trash had been collected, broken furniture repaired. To Alanya's eyes, it looked almost like the home in which she had grown up. Considering that she had, very recently, been worried that she would never again see anything beyond the log walls of Koronaka, she was thrilled to be back. She couldn't wait to get in touch with her friends, now that ownership was settled, and let them know she was home.

Arigan found her when she went to the room that had been hers. It was obvious that Rangers had stayed here—it smelled like unwashed men, and the white-washed walls were still grimy. She didn't like the idea of taking over her father's room, especially since she knew Lupinius had done the same. But she might not have much choice.

"Lady Alanya?" Arigan said from the doorway. The old woman had been a nanny to Alanya from the time of her birth, then Donial. She had been kept on as a cook when they were too old to need nannies anymore.

"Yes, Arigan?"

"Welcome home, Lady," she said. She crossed the room to give Alanya a frail, tentative hug. Her frock was nearly as gray as her hair, and she wore an apron that had been white once, but held the stains of a thousand meals prepared. "I am so glad to see you."

"Not as glad as I am, Arigan," Alanya swore. "I had thought I would never see you, or this place, again."

"I know your father wanted you both to have it," Arigan said. Her eyes were moist, and Alanya thought, with some surprise, that the old woman might weep. "When Lupinius came, I thought the worst had happened."

Alanya sat down on the room's only bed. "It had," she said. "He killed Father, Arigan. Or had him killed. I am sure of it. I just know not how to prove it, now that he cannot confess his crime."

"That does not surprise me," Arigan said. "He always did have a dislike for his brother. Envious of the things Invictus earned, but not willing to work hard enough to make his own way in the world."

"I never saw that before," Alanya admitted.

"You were too young," Arigan told her. Her tone was hushed, so that Alanya had to strain to hear her. "By the time you were old enough to have noticed, Lupinius had moved away. Gone to seek his fortune, he said. More like gone to find someone fool enough to give him one."

"He very nearly did," Alanya replied. "Or someone he could steal from, anyway. He even stole from me."

Arigan *tsk*ed and shook her head. "I am not at all surprised," she said again. "Nothing about him surprises me. Did he take more from you than this house and land?"

"Oh, yes," Alanya answered. "He took a mirror Father had given me, my mother's old mirror."

"I meant to ask you about that," Arigan said, as if she had just remembered. "Your mother's mirror. A very precious item, indeed. Do you have it now?"

"I got it back," Alanya said. She didn't go into detail about how. "There is one other thing I have not found, though. A crown, belonging to a friend."

"I have seen no crown," Arigan said. "But about that mirror . . . did your father ever tell you about its properties?"

Alanya was confused. "Properties?"

"There is more to that mirror than meets the eye," Arigan said.

"He suggested that it might be magic in some way," Alanya admitted. "Cheveray told me the same thing. But I have no idea what is magic about it."

Arigan came closer, kneeling, with evident pain, beside the bed so she could lower her voice even more. "It is magical, all right," the old woman said. "That's why it has been handed down, generation to generation, within this family."

"But we are not . . . we aren't a family of wizards or witches, are we?"

"Not at all," Arigan assured her. "But one of your ancestors did one a favor, long ago. That favor was returned, with the gift of the mirror. The mirror that now belongs to you, along with that gift."

"But . . . what good is its magic if no one knows what it does, or how to work it?" Alanya wondered aloud.

"Who said that no one does?"

It took a moment for her meaning to sink in. "Do you?"

"Aye, child," Arigan said. Her cheeks were flushed with excitement. "Your mother showed me, years ago. I never really knew why. Now I think it was so that I might show you, when the time came."

Alanya felt a rush of excitement, as if she were being initiated into some great mystery. "I have it in my bags," she said. She had very few personal possessions. But she and Donial still had the horses Kral had acquired for them, and they'd loaded their things onto those mounts for the move. Her bags had been brought to her room by one of the staff, at her request. She went to the one in which she thought she had stashed the mirror and dug around until she found it.

When she brought it back, she knelt on the floor beside the old woman and reverently laid the precious thing on her bed, glass side up. "Here it is."

Arigan sighed. "I would recognize that anywhere," she said. "Even after a hundred hundred years, if I lived so long."

"I hope you do," Alanya said. "But . . . how does it work? What is it supposed to do?"

Before Arigan could answer, Donial strode into the room and flopped down on the bed. "Wondered where you were," he said. "What's going on?"

"Arigan is telling me about mother's mirror," Alanya explained. "It really is magic."

Donial sat up, his interest piqued. "It isn't."

"Oh, but it is," Arigan countered. "Very much so."

"What does it do?" Donial demanded.

"I was just getting to that," Arigan told him. "Because it is a looking glass, its magic is tied to its natural function. In this case, if you look into it and speak a name three times—and if that person has ever looked into the mirror—it will show you his or her image."

"Even if they are not looking in it now?" Donial asked.

"If they were looking in it now, it would just be a normal mirror, silly," Alanya pointed out. "That would not be magic, would it?"

"Anyone who has *ever* looked into it," Arigan assured them.

"So . . . I could see Mother?" Alanya asked.

Arigan put a long, bony finger to her wrinkled lips. "You could," she said. "But when viewing the dead, you will not see them as they are now. You will see the last time she gazed into the glass."

That seemed fine to Alanya. Her mother had been dead for years, and now she would be nothing but bones. But still, she wanted to see what the woman had looked like, to see if it matched her memory, her imagination. She pictured her mother as almost impossibly beautiful. Could it really be true?

"All right, then," she said. She stared into the glass until her own reflection swam, unfocused, before her eyes. "Martene, Martene, Martene."

Seconds passed, and nothing happened. Alanya waited, disappointment rising in her like a tide. The mirror wasn't magic after all. Not that she had really expected anything different. Everyone heard about magic, knew some sorcerer or other by name and reputation, if not personally. But no one she knew seemed to have any genuine experience with it. It was something in stories, not something that touched the lives of people like her.

She let her eyes focus again on her own reflection, then . . .

. . . and then, it was not her reflection at all. It was a woman with golden hair, like hers, and eyes of the bluest blue. But it was not Alanya.

For a moment, she wondered if the other woman in the glass could see her. But, of course, she couldn't. Alanya was just seeing what her mother had seen the last time she had looked into the glass. She squinted, she poked at the corner of her lips, a bit thinner than Alanya's own, she tilted her head to examine her own neck.

It was Mother, as clear as day! The magic did work, after all!

Alanya wanted to cry out, to speak to her. She showed Donial, who stared, wide-eyed. "That's Mother?"

Alanya knew his memory of their mother was more vague than her own. "Yes," she said. "Yes, that is Mother. Absolutely."

"She is so pretty," Donial said.

"Isn't she?" Arigan responded. "Like her daughter."

Alanya felt suddenly embarrassed. Yes, she did look quite a bit like her mother. But her mother's face was more mature, more elegant in some way. She felt as if her own had not fully formed yet.

Before she could say anything more, the image faded away, and the mirror returned to reflecting those things before it. "She is gone."

"You get only a glimpse," Arigan explained. "Especially of the dead."

"But with the living," Donial began. Alanya could tell by his face that he had an idea. "It will show them as they are now?"

"Exactly."

"Alanya," Donial said anxiously. "Ask it to show us Kral!"

She understood at once. She had shown Kral the mirror, that fateful day when Donial had discovered them together. He had gazed into it on that occasion, which should, if Arigan was correct, be enough to let its magic work on him. If it would show Kral as he was at that moment, perhaps it would also show enough of his surroundings for them to be able to figure out where he was. If, by some horrible quirk of fate, he had been killed, she hoped they would be able to tell that as well.

She looked deep into the mirror again, as if trying to see the glass surface beneath her reflection, and spoke his name three times.

A few moments passed, as before, and then, with no warning, she saw an image of Kral.

He wasn't looking into the mirror, as her mother had seemed to be. Instead, the vantage point was from a foot or more away from him, as if Alanya,

Donial, and Arigan were unseen viewers, observing him. He looked tired. His dark hair was matted, strands of it hanging loosely around his face. He appeared to be hunched over, sitting or squatting, in a dark place.

"What is that behind him?" Donial wondered.

Alanya had been closely examining her friend's weary face, without looking at the surroundings. Donial was right—there was something visible in the darkness—four bands of light, evenly spaced.

"A window of some kind?" Arigan offered.

"Those are . . . those are bars!" Donial said excitedly. "He is in some kind of cage."

"Or a cell," Alanya added. "Perhaps he was arrested."

"That would make sense," Donial said. "It would explain why he never made it back to Cheveray's."

Alanya knew that seeing Kral's surroundings could be a major breakthrough. Cheveray had been making discreet inquiries, but without any certain knowledge of the young Pict's whereabouts, his efforts had necessarily been widespread. Now he could narrow them.

Somewhere, likely here in Tarantia, Kral was being held prisoner.

All they had to do now was find out where—then figure out a way to get him out!

6

CONOR KNEW THE youngsters were counting on
him to find their friend's missing crown—although
from its description, he couldn't imagine why anyone
would want it. And he knew he would not be paid any
more until he did so.

What he didn't know was how to go about it.

He'd been popular with his fellow villagers back in
Taern—feared, respected, and liked in more or less
equal proportions. But he had also been curious about
life outside Cimmeria. As stories about Conan's ex-
ploits filtered out of the warmer lands to the south—and
especially after he had become king in Aquilonia—that
curiosity had become overwhelming.

Anxious to see what Conan had found in the
wide world, Conor had left home and made his own

trek, south to Tarantia. Here, he had found friendly, voluptuous women who were drawn to big, muscular men like him—although his appeal seemed to fade the emptier his purse became. He also found occasional opportunities to replenish that purse, most of them illegal and a number of them dangerous as well.

Now an opportunity had come along that seemed to be legal, and could—if these teens were really as wealthy as they seemed—wind up filling his purse. All he had to do was figure out which thief, of the hundreds or maybe thousands who inhabited Tarantia, had stolen the odd head ornament.

Dusk was settling over the big city, softening shadows before night thickened them, and drawing the night-dwellers out onto the streets. Fathers hurried home to be with their families. Thieves, cutthroats, and whores emerged from their dens. Lamps were being lit all over the city.

It was the time of night Conor liked best in Tarantia. At home, the fall of dusk drove people into their huts to wait for the sun's return. But here it just signaled a change in who was out and about. One never needed to be alone in Tarantia; someplace in the city there was always someone to pass the time with.

With the thieves out, maybe he could get started on his appointed task.

He stepped onto a narrow side street and waited in the gathering gloom. It didn't take long for a man to start down the street, a big fellow with a surprisingly light step and a rolling gait. He wore a narrow-bladed sword at his left hip, and a dagger on his right, ready to be cross-drawn.

Instead of letting him have that chance, Conor waited, motionless, until the man had passed, then stepped out close behind him. "You a thief?" he asked quietly.

"Could be," the man asked, startled but covering it well. "Why do you ask?"

"I seek something stolen of late," Conor replied. "A barbaric crown, of bones and teeth. Have you heard of it?"

"Me, I specialize in gems from the boudoirs of noblewomen," the man said. He still hadn't turned around, but his posture was tense and coiled, ready for anything. "A crown such as you describe would not interest me in the least."

Conor felt a sudden, inexplicable rage boil up in him. "That is not what I asked!" He swung at the back of the thief's head, a glancing blow that nonetheless knocked the other man sprawling in the middle of the street. "I asked if you had heard anything about it."

The thief worked his way to a sitting position, rubbing the back of his head and glaring angrily at Conor. "No," he declared flatly. "I have not."

"If you do," Conor suggested, "find me and tell me. My name is Conor, of Cimmeria. I would find the crown I have described, if it is yet in Tarantia."

"I . . . I will ask around," the thief volunteered. "Just don't hit me again."

Conor folded his arms across his massive chest and nodded. "Very well," he said. The thief scuttled backward, away from Conor, then rose and hurried away.

That gave Conor an idea for how to go about his task. Before being swatted, the fellow had been unwilling to cooperate at all. After, he had offered to help.

Conor could happily knock around thieves all evening. One of them, surely, would know something about the missing crown.

He started for a tavern where he knew he could find some likely candidates.

FOUR HOURS LATER, Conor pounded on the door of a second-floor apartment in which a thief named Tremont was said to live.

The apartment, coincidentally, was only a couple of blocks from the basement where Conor himself had found lodging, shortly after arriving in Tarantia. The building was ramshackle and pungent, and there seemed to be as many people sitting or sleeping in the hallway as inside the apartments themselves. Several scratched at themselves, some even in their sleep. Conor supposed that meant that this fellow Tremont was a more successful thief than these others, who huddled against the walls, dressed in rags, quaking with fear at Conor's approach.

There was no response to his pounding, so he opened the door. Unbolted, it swung open easily when he worked the latch. As he stepped inside, the stink of rotten food assailed his nostrils, and through an open window, a single shaft of moonlight illuminated a trembling form, lying on a bed.

"You," Conor said. "You are Tremont?"

The person on the bed said something, but Conor couldn't make it out. He moved closer, his hand resting lightly on the hilt of his broadsword, ready to draw and strike at a moment's notice. His sandals stuck to something covering the floor, and he knew at once, by the smell, that it was blood.

As he neared, he saw a man under a threadbare blanket, shivering with such ferocity he was practically vibrating. The man was skinny, with long hair sweat-plastered to a face that looked like horses had stampeded across it. "You are Tremont?" Conor asked again.

"I am," the man said, his voice barely a whisper.

"I am told you stole a crown, made of bones and teeth," Conor said. "Where is it?"

"G-gone," the shivering man managed.

"Gone where?" Conor demanded. "You sold it?"

The man on the bed might have been shaking his head, but with his trembling it was hard to tell. "What, then?" Conor wanted to know.

"St-Stygians," Tremont said. It almost seemed that the thought of them made him shiver harder. "Priests, in black robes. Th . . . three of them. They took it."

"Do you know where these Stygians might have gone?" Conor asked.

Tremont shook his head again.

Conor leaned closer, trying to scare the injured man with his sheer size and presence. "I need the crown," he said. He caught a whiff of Tremont's odor and realized that the spoiled food smell in the place came from him. The thief was dying, and fast.

"T-teeth," the thief mumbled.

"Yes, it has teeth," Conor said impatiently. "What about them?"

"The crown . . . is not whole . . ." Tremont explained. "I sold some teeth."

"You sold them? To who?"

Tremont hesitated, then a violent paroxysm gripped him. Conor was afraid he would die before he was able to speak again. But after a few moments it passed, and Tremont, face wet with new perspiration, managed to speak again. "A . . . a man named . . . Chellus."

Conor nodded. He had heard of Chellus, though he had never seen the man. Rumor was that Chellus would buy anything stolen, no matter how hard it might be to resell. He paid low prices for everything and made his money by purchasing the occasional genuinely valuable item from thieves already indebted to him for taking less pricey items off their hands.

Maybe Chellus still had the teeth. And maybe, now that Conor knew where they were, he himself could get his hands on them. He didn't know precisely what they were or what they might portend, but if Stygian priests were after the crown, then it was likely that someone would pay a decent price for the missing parts of it. He decided he would have to pay a visit to Chellus soon.

He had heard enough, he thought. Tremont was going to die at any time, and he didn't want to be around when that happened. The place stank enough already.

Without bothering to thank the shivering thief, he walked out of the man's apartment, leaving the door wide open.

The sooner someone found him, the sooner they would get his body out of the apartment. Maybe if it was cleaned up, it wouldn't be half-bad.

Conor wouldn't have minded moving out of his basement, not at all. There could be some real benefits to being on the second floor.

He would have to keep an eye on the place.

HIS HANDS CLASPED before him, Cheveray nodded and smiled. "I have some good news, children," he said. He sat in a chair, with his cane balanced across his knees. "Very good news indeed."

Having sent word, via a servant, to Cheveray about what the mirror had revealed, Donial and Alanya had spent their first night in their childhood home, feeling a warmth and sense of comfort long denied them. But with morning, the urgency to find Kral had reestablished itself, and they had returned to Cheveray's house to discuss what they had seen in the magic mirror.

"What is it?" Alanya wanted to know.

"Because of what you saw in your mother's mirror," Cheveray revealed, "I had a place to start that I had not before. During the night, agents of mine asked some pointed questions, and we have located your friend."

"You found him?" Donial asked in stunned surprise. "Where is he?"

"We didn't even know what prison it was," Alanya reminded them.

"True," Cheveray acknowledged. "But we knew more than we did before, and were able to focus our search. He is being held in a city prison, accused of having killed an Aquilonian soldier, in addition to murdering your uncle and Rufio, his Ranger guard."

"Murder?" Donial asked. But he quickly remembered that Kral had done just that, on numerous occasions, back in Koronaka. Why should it surprise him now? He was, after all, a savage, who didn't cleave to the same customs as civilized folk.

"Aye," Cheveray confirmed. "A serious charge indeed."

"Then . . . how can we get him out?" Alanya demanded. "We cannot just leave him there. We know he did not kill Lupinius or Rufio. Have you asked King Conan for help?"

There had been a time when Donial had not been so sure that prison wasn't the best place for him. After all, it was Alanya, not he, who had made fast friends with the Pict. What difference to him if Kral stayed in jail? Alanya would grieve, but she would get over it. Even Donial would miss him to some extent, having enjoyed his company on their trip to Tarantia. Not nearly as much as his sister would, but he had come to respect the savage's primitive outlook on things.

"That, I fear, is where I have run into a stone wall," Cheveray said. "Since he is accused of killing one of the King's soldiers, I do not dare appeal to Conan. And the only way to prove that he did not commit the murders at your house would be for you both to admit that you were also there. Then, of course, you might all be charged. The other crime of which he is accused—having been committed before several witnesses, soldiers and Rangers alike—is perhaps more troubling still. There's little doubt that he is guilty. From the sound of things, I suspect he was simply trying to escape and saw those soldiers as a threat. I understand his actions. But you must understand that the authorities have every intention of seeing him executed for it."

"Then . . . then it's hopeless?" Alanya asked. Donial was afraid his sister would start to cry.

"I did not say that." Cheveray tapped his long fingers on the cane. "Anything can be done, Alanya," he assured the girl. "If one has the will—and sometimes, the means—anything at all can be accomplished. It is simply a matter of how hard one is willing to work for it."

"We will do whatever we have to," Alanya vowed. "We cannot just let Kral rot in there or die on the headsman's block."

"Prison is hard for any free man," Cheveray agreed. "For a young man raised in the open wilderness, probably harder still."

Alanya was about to respond when one of Cheveray's servants interrupted. "A visitor, sir," the old man said. "For the young people."

Donial felt a surge of certainty. *Kral!* he thought. *Somehow, it must be Kral.*

He practically leapt from his chair. Alanya followed closely, and Cheveray, slowed by his infirmity, hobbled along behind.

But when they reached the doorway, it was Conor who stood there, not Kral. Donial felt a wave of disappointment, but a shallow one. Conor wouldn't be here if he hadn't learned *something*.

"What news?" he asked.

Conor waited until all were gathered in the entry before answering. "I found the man who stole the crown from your uncle. His name is Tremont, and he was near death—is likely dead by now, I'd wager."

"So you have it?" Alanya asked anxiously.

"No," Conor replied. "Someone stole it from the thief. Three Stygian priests, he said. Doubtless the thing is already in transit back to that dark and mysterious land."

"Stygians, eh?" Cheveray pursed his lips. "Bad news, that."

"Bad, yes," Conor agreed. Donial thought the big man almost shivered. "Those Sons of Set make me nervous."

"Understandable," Cheveray said. "Why, when I was in Stygia . . . but you don't want to hear about that now. Young man, you have done excellent work."

"But we still know not where the crown is," Donial protested.

"True," Cheveray admitted. "But we know where it is headed. Nothing we can do at this moment to stop it, I'd wager."

"Anyway, Conor," Alanya put in, "we have something else to deal with right now. We have discovered where our friend is."

"And he's in prison," Donial added. Perhaps this

new information could help alleviate the suspicion that Kral had had anything to do with their uncle's death, or Rufio's. But how could they present it to the authorities? Mitra only knew what laws Conor had broken to discover the thief's identity.

"That is correct," said Cheveray. He looked the big Cimmerian up and down, as if measuring him for a suit of armor—or a shroud. "And you might be able to help us get him out."

"I . . . I have some other pressing business," Conor hedged.

"It need not take much time," Cheveray said. "And we could definitely use a big, strong fellow like you. You would be a huge help."

"You agreed to help us get Kral back," Alanya reminded the barbarian. "This is part of the job. We still need to get the crown, but we are not going to Stygia without Kral."

"That's right," Donial seconded. He still had no idea what Cheveray's plan might be, or how Conor would fit in. But he didn't want Conor simply to walk away if there was, in fact, a plan to be put into action. "You have to help."

Conor looked uncomfortable. Donial could tell there was someplace else he'd rather be. But finally, apparently accepting that he had already agreed, he gave in. "Very well," he said. "I will do what I can. What is your plan?"

7

KRAL HAD NO intention of peacefully meeting a headsman's axe.

As long as he drew breath, he would fight for life. According to Carillus, the jailer, his appointment with the executioner was not far off. He would be transferred from the city jail into a military one, which would be much more rigid and severe, and it was from there that he would be taken when the time came. So Kral was determined to increase his efforts to break free of the dark prison, before he was moved.

Every night, he tried the door. It was always locked. Carillus never unlocked it—he just slid food trays in through a small opening in the door and occasionally demanded that Kral's toilet pail be passed out the same way. The opening was too small for Kral to squeeze through, though he had tried. And Kral had not been allowed out of the cell once since he had been locked in. Totlio told him that in years gone by, prisoners had been chained to the walls within their cells. As part of his efforts at modernizing Aquilonia, King Conan had done away with that practice.

So Kral tried the door, testing to see if it was unlocked, even though he knew it wasn't. Then he tried the bars set into the thick wood of the door, but they were solid, sturdy. He could not loosen them or break the wood. That done, he turned his attention to the walls. He had guessed, and Totlio confirmed, that the cells were underground. Even if he could dig through one of the cell walls, he figured he would only find earth behind it, or another cell. He would have to dig up and out like a rabbit, and it couldn't possibly be done in one night.

The only advantage he had was that at night there was no jailer down in the cell area with them. When Carillus left, locking a door at the top of the curved staircase, the prisoners were alone down here. That was the worst time, for Kral. Several of the prisoners seemed to have slipped over the edge of madness, and at night they laughed, sang, raved, and danced about in their cells like the lunatics they were. During the day, he could at least spend time talking to Carillus and Totlio, and the others, the mad ones, were quieter.

At night he could devote himself to trying to find a way out of his cell, but each time he did, he reached the same conclusion.

It was hopeless. He could not break the door, he could not pass through the walls.

If he was going to get out, someone would have to open the door for him. It was as simple as that.

Since there were only three people in Tarantia who might care that he was down here, he sincerely doubted that would happen. Until, that was, they came to take him to the chopping block.

Each night, Kral tried the door, tried the walls, just in case. Then he exercised, doing what he could, in the cramped space, to keep his muscles strong.

When they came for him, they wouldn't find a docile victim, weakened by his time in the cell.

They would find a Pictish warrior, ready for battle.

WHEN THE JAILER looked up, his face registered surprise at the sight before him. Well it might. He could not have remembered another time when two teenagers, a bent, humpbacked old man in a voluminous purple cloak, and a giant Cimmerian had entered his building together. They came as evening fell, just after the time when the downstairs guard had retired for the night, leaving only him, upstairs to watch over things. That was considered sufficient protection, as the building itself was within a greater

compound. Only people who were supposed to be
here could pass through the gates into the compound,
but fortunately, Cheveray's connections, combined
with judiciously applied bribery, gained them en-
trance. The gate through which they had come was
unguarded, and would remain so for another hour,
Cheveray had been promised. None would see them
enter or leave.

The prison building was solid, nearly impenetrable, Alanya guessed. Which only made sense. Its
walls were two feet thick, built of solid stone blocks.
There were only a few windows, too small for any
creature larger than a bird or a mouse to pass through,
and set high in the wall. Its sole door was wood rein-
forced with iron panels and hardware. To that door,
however, Cheveray had somehow acquired a key. So
instead of knocking and alerting whatever guards
waited on the inside, Cheveray had simply unlocked
the door, and they all walked in together.

That was when the guard looked up from the
bench on which he sat. "What . . . what do you want?"
he demanded. "How did you get in here?"

"The door was unlocked," Cheveray lied.

"It certainly was not!" the guard insisted. He was
a stocky man, with a florid face and a thick brush of
dark hair on top of his round head. His sword and
helmet sat on the bench near him, but not immediately to hand. Obviously he had not been expecting
visitors. On the wall beside the bench was a rack

containing a variety of keys and a huge wooden whistle that a guard would have used to summon aid if need be. A single, heavy door led away from the room—undoubtedly the door to the cells below.

"Do you think I could have opened it otherwise?" Cheveray asked. "Look at me."

The guard did just that. Alanya realized that Cheveray had played it just right. He had entered first, after unlocking the door with his key. So his was the only hand the guard had seen on the door.

"It is not supposed to be unlocked," the guard said. He rose, but still didn't make for his weapon.

"I am sure not," Cheveray agreed. "Most dangerous, I should expect. You should be more careful."

"I . . . I am certain I locked it," the guard blustered. "Must have been someone else."

Alanya and the others had been watching the building from a nearby alleyway for almost an hour. Whoever had supplied Cheveray the key had also told him about the schedule the guards kept. They knew the other guards had all gone, so this guard might be able to convince himself that it had been one of his fellows leaving who had failed to secure the door.

"Be that as it may," the guard said, regaining his composure somewhat, "you are not supposed to be in here. What do you want?"

"Simply some help with directions," Cheveray said. "We seem to have gotten lost." He fished a rolled map from beneath his cloak and approached the guard, unrolling it as he did. "If you could just show me—"

"Out!" the guard cried. "I will show you nothing. Leave now, or I'll arrest you myself."

Cheveray didn't stop, however. He couldn't have looked very threatening, with his twisted form and the cane he used to walk. As he neared the guard, he allowed the map to unroll completely, and he held it up before the guard's face, almost enveloping the man with it.

That was when Conor rushed past Donial and Alanya. With the guard distracted, his weapon and whistle both forgotten, and the map carefully positioned to indicate his target, he charged the guard, swinging one giant fist directly into the guard's chin.

The guard let out a grunt of pain. He tore at the map with both hands, trying to move it. Cheveray released it then and backed out of the way. Conor drove his left fist low, into the guard's midsection, and followed with another right to the man's jaw. The guard sank back to the bench, dazed or unconscious, as the map rustled to the floor.

"The keys, children," Cheveray said, urgency in his voice. Alanya and Donial grabbed keys from the rack beside the addled guard. They took turns fitting them into the door, until one of them turned, and the lock released. It still required both of them pulling on it to open the door.

"You will likely need keys downstairs as well," Cheveray reminded them. "Take them all, in case. And have a care!"

The plan was for both Cheveray and Conor to stay upstairs—Conor in case the guard came around, and Cheveray because once he got down, he wouldn't be able to climb quickly. Which left it to Alanya and Donial to descend into the dark, find which cell was Kral's, and let him out. Alanya was scared at what she might see down there—and what might see her. But she owed Kral, and they had not come this far just to walk away. She steeled her courage, got a good grip on her share of keys, and started down the stairs. Only two torches, widely spaced, lit the way.

"Who's there?" a strange voice called up from below. "It isn't time, isn't time!"

"A madman," Donial whispered. "Place is probably crawling with them."

"That doesn't help," Alanya replied. She wanted to find Kral quickly, didn't want to think about who else might be locked down there.

"We could call him," Donial suggested.

She paused on the stairs. She could see a line of cell doors, but the torchlight didn't penetrate the cells themselves. Even if she was willing to stick her face right up against the bars, she wouldn't be able to see Kral. "I guess we must," she agreed.

"Kral!" Donial spoke his name in a loud whisper,

as if everyone in the cells wouldn't be able to hear it anyway. "Kral, where are you?"

"Right here!" Kral's voice came from a cell just three doors away from the staircase, then his hand waved through the bars in his door. "I'm in here!"

"We're coming, Kral!" Alanya called. "We have keys, worry not. You will be out in a minute."

"Take me, too!" another voice shouted. It sounded like it came from the cell next to Kral's. "Take me, boy! I have been here too long. I would see the sun again, ere I die."

"No, Totlio," Kral said. "It is too dangerous."

"Nothing is more dangerous than staying in here," the man Kral called Totlio pleaded. "Please, take me with you!"

By that time Alanya had gained the door to Kral's cell. She tried key after key in its lock, to no avail. Kral came to the bars, but she could barely make out his face in the gloom. He smiled maniacally at her. "I suppose we could free him," Kral suggested. "I doubt he can run very fast. Maybe when they realize that we are both missing, they will go after him first, as an easier target."

"Donial, try your keys!" Alanya urged. "I'll try his door," she said.

When she stopped in front of that other door, the man inside started crying and laughing and praying. He made Alanya nervous, but she worked her way through the keys. When she found the one that opened the lock, she paused and waited for Donial. She didn't want to let the old man out before Kral was released, just in case he was less harmless than Kral seemed to think.

But then Donial got Kral's door open, and the Pict enveloped her brother in a hurried embrace as he exited his cell. She opened the old man's at the same time, then immediately turned to Kral. Another embrace, this one held a moment longer, and the three of them started up the staircase. Behind them, the old man was only just coming out of his cell.

Upstairs, she saw that Conor had hit the guard again. He was now slumped on the floor, blood running from nose and mouth. Cheveray waited near the door to the street, his eyes bright with anxiety and excitement. When he saw Kral appear, he raised his cane in triumph. "Excellent! Come, boy! Your friends have been working hard for your release, and there is much news to share!"

Alanya saw Kral hesitate momentarily when he spotted Conor. Cimmerians and Picts were natural enemies, she knew. "He is with us," she assured him. "He helped get you out."

"Did you tell me he was a Pict?" Conor asked, as they left the guardhouse.

"Yes," Alanya assured him. "You were drunk and might not remember. But we did."

On the street, Kral's head swiveled this way and that, looking at his rescuers with amazement. Finally,

Alanya took his hand and led him into the shadows, toward the abandoned gate through which they had entered the compound. "We'll tell you everything," she promised. "Just not here."

They were two blocks away, and running as fast as they could—Conor carrying Cheveray as easily as a sack of flour—when the alarm whistle finally blew.

8

CHELLUS WORKED OUT of the back of a little shop that specialized in inexpensive jewelry, mostly for women and girls. Glass cut to look like diamonds, or stained to resemble emeralds, rubies, or jade. Common metals polished and colored to pass for gold or silver. Every now and then, the real thing would fall into his hands, primarily through the side business he ran out of his cramped back room when there were no paying customers in the front. When that happened, he would move the item through some other contact, even though it meant sharing a cut of the profits, rather than sell it through the shop, thereby drawing attention to both the low prices and low quality of his phonies.

Every thief in town knew of Chellus, as he and his

fellow purveyors of stolen goods were an important aspect of plying their trade. So Conor had heard stories and knew where to find the man. He figured Tremont wouldn't have given up his name if he hadn't known he was dying, with nothing left to lose.

Conor hung around outside until he knew the shop was empty. Then he entered casually, as if just wandering in from the street. After a few moments, Chellus emerged from the back room. He was a portly fellow, bald on top with a fringe of red hair around his cranium, wearing a gray shirt and breeches with a black apron over them. "Looking for a gift for a special lady?" he asked.

Conor had rehearsed his lines. He touched his purse—laden with the coins the siblings had paid him for helping to free their friend—and said, "No, I am looking for someone who might be interested in buying things without asking where they came from."

Chellus took a step back, wiped both his palms on his apron, and wrinkled his forehead. "And what makes you think you'd find such a person here?"

Conor shrugged. "Friends tell each other things," he said. "Your reputation as an honest broker of found things spreads far and wide."

"Found things," Chellus echoed with a low chuckle. "I like that." He waved Conor toward his back room. "Join me in here, where it's private."

Conor threaded his way between display cases packed with fake jewelry and through a curtained doorway. Chellus's back room was crowded with the tools of his trade—jewelry-making equipment, cases of raw materials, cloth bags stuffed with things Conor couldn't begin to imagine. There was precious little space for people in the room, so Conor found himself standing very close to the other man. Too close to use his sword, he noted.

But rather than waste any more time here, he gave Chellus a wide, menacing grin. "I lied," he said. "I want the teeth you bought from Tremont."

"Teeth?" Chellus repeated. "Why would I buy teeth?"

"I know not." Conor put a hand on Chellus's shoulder and gave it a firm squeeze. Chellus winced under the pressure. "I care not. I just want them."

Sweat beaded on the merchant's forehead. He looked like he wanted to protest, but Conor just kept squeezing, harder and harder. Chellus's legs began to tremble. "All right," he said, blowing out with a fierce exhalation. "All right, you're damnably strong. I've got the teeth still—merely took them from Tremont as a favor, and I have no idea who would buy them. You are welcome to them."

Conor released him. Chellus turned to a faded wooden cabinet, sliding open one of the drawers. He rummaged around for a minute, then came out bearing a small cloth bag. He opened the bag's drawstring and dumped the contents into his hand, holding it out for Conor's perusal.

Two teeth, as the children had described. They looked like the teeth of a bear, but they were far larger than any he had ever seen. "Good," he said.

Chellus put them back in the bag and handed it over to Conor, who closed his hand around it. "I should make you pay me what I paid him," Chellus threatened.

"Feel free to try," Conor replied.

Chellus scowled. "Just go, barbarian. Never show yourself here again."

"I don't plan to," Conor said. He turned, not afraid to show the merchant his back, and walked out of the shop. At the doorway, he saw two young women, in their twenties, he guessed, about to enter.

"Don't bother," he told them. "Everything inside is fake, and the owner is a fraud."

The ladies glanced at each other, back at Conor, and smiled. One of them thanked him, and he walked away, clutching his prize, glad he'd been able to send Chellus that parting gift as well.

Though he had the teeth, he still didn't know what they were or how to turn them into treasure. But the fact that Stygian priests wanted them was a good indicator of their value. He also had the coins he had been paid for helping free the Pict from jail. It was a far cry from being wealthy, but it was more money than Conor had ever known all at once.

In Tarantia, it was still precious little. Home in Cimmeria, though, it would go far.

He figured he had seen enough of the civilized world. Conan had been able to make a home in the city, and that was fine for him. But Conor would never be completely happy away from Cimmeria's icy canyons and steep cliffs. He suspected that Conan had been made soft by his life here—"civilized," with all that entailed. He doubted that any Cimmerian could have maintained his barbaric edge, living here for so long. Conan's legend was well-known, and people said he was still a lion in combat. But that was combat against other civilized folks, not against real warriors.

Conor refused to let that happen to him. And if he left immediately, he wouldn't be sucked into some ill-fated misadventure in Stygia—a place he had no interest whatsoever in visiting.

As he ambled down the street away from Chellus's shop, he kept an eye open for a horse to steal.

KANILLA REY WAS furious. He knew that letting his anger control him was a bad idea, but he couldn't help it. Instead of walking, he stomped. He slammed his fist into every flat surface he saw. He fumed.

Shehkmi Al Nasir had been his ally and friend. As close to a friend as another wizard could ever be, at any rate. Now, the Stygian had betrayed him. According to Gorian, Stygian priests had stolen the Pictish crown right out from under him.

Betrayal of that sort could not go unanswered.

Kanilla Rey looked at the men Gorian had rounded up. Twenty of them, they filled the street behind his home. They were a motley bunch: mercenaries, mostly past their prime, who would work for the wage Kanilla Rey was offering. One of them must have been in his sixties, with arms so thin and wrinkled the sorcerer doubted he could lift his own sword. Kanilla Rey pointed at him. "You, get out," he said. The old man looked like he wanted to complain, but he lowered his head and left without argument.

The rest looked battle-tested, at least. There was not a one of them into whose hands Kanilla Rey would put his own life, but he would be staying behind in Tarantia. Gorian, who had worked for him several times, and was unknowingly slipping closer and closer to being under Kanilla Rey's complete control, would be in charge of the mission, reporting back to Kanilla Rey.

If anything happened to Gorian, it would be a loss—he had invested considerable time and effort in the man. But it wouldn't be like entrusting his own safety to this bunch.

"You lot," he said to the assembled group. "You know to where you journey?"

"Stygia," one answered.

"Hell," another said, to general merriment.

"Possibly both," Kanilla Rey said. "But Stygia first. You will take your orders from Gorian, there, the man who brought you together." He pointed toward his agent, lest any of the men who were drunk when Gorian had found them forget to whom they owed their enlistment.

The mercenaries eyed Gorian, then launched into a series of questions about when and how often they would be paid, whether they would get to share in any booty, and so on. Kanilla Rey let Gorian answer while he regarded his little troop.

Nineteen, now that the old man had gone. Plus Gorian, and Sullas, the other man who had survived the Stygian priests. Some of them would doubtless die before they even reached the desert kingdom, and many more would do so when they went up against the forces of Shehkmi al Nasir.

Kanilla Rey would be helping from afar, when he could. If he could afford a bigger force, he would send it. But that would take time and treasure, more than he could put his hands on at the moment. Somehow, they would just have to get his crown back.

The thing had power, and he wanted it. While he waited he would do more research, consult the most ancient tomes available, until he learned just what it was and how to use it. Once he had it in his hands, Shehkmi al Nasir would be no bigger threat than a mosquito.

He looked forward to that day, and smiled.

•   •   •

SITTING INSIDE THE home that now belonged to Alanya and Donial was very different from sneaking around it in the dark of night, avoiding the authorities. Kral was impressed with the size and luxury of the place. It even had indoor toilets, of all things! Like Cheveray's house, it promised a life he couldn't see himself ever living, but he understood why these more civilized people would appreciate it. At any rate, he was glad for Alanya's sake that she was finally home, in the place she had always loved.

Not that it looked as if she would be staying long. Having broken him out of prison, suspicion would fall on her and Donial. They had to get out of town for a time. And they had someplace to go, since according to the Cimmerian, the Teeth were on their way to Stygia.

They had scrolls unrolled on a table, maps detailing the path they must take. Kral wasn't used to maps, but he could compare the distance between where Donial said Koronaka was, and Tarantia, and easily tell that it was even farther to Stygia. Almost twice as far, in fact.

And the Stygians had a head start.

"It would take us weeks," Kral pointed out. "If our horses even survive the trip."

"But we will not go on horseback," Donial countered.

"How, then?"

Alanya traced her delicate finger along a thin line

on the map. "This is the Tybor River," she said. "We will travel overland to the river, where we can book passage on one of the ships that ply its length." She indicated on the map where the river opened out onto the ocean. "Here, it is only a short ocean voyage, hugging the coast, until the mouth of the River Styx."

"Do we know where in Stygia to look for the Teeth?" Kral asked.

"Not precisely," Donial admitted. "Conor did not learn that much. We will just have to figure that part out when we get there."

Kral glanced at the map again. Stygia looked like a big place.

But he trusted Alanya and Donial. They knew more about the world than he did. If they thought they could find the Teeth in Stygia, he was more than willing to go along with them. He was just thankful they were willing to make the trip in the first place, and equally appreciative that they had made the effort to break him out of that prison. He could hardly believe his luck—that he, a barbarian Pict, would have made such good friends among the hated Aquilonians. It wasn't something he could ever have predicted, but he was glad it had happened. Now, they were going to brave the dark, mysterious land of Stygia at his side.

Especially surprising, because after all, the Teeth was his responsibility, not theirs. He was one of the last surviving members of the Bear Clan, appointed

so long ago to safeguard the sacred crown. He was
the one who needed to find the object and return it to
its place in the Guardian's cave.

And every day that passed before he did so, he was
convinced, only brought the Picts closer to disaster.

9

THE *RESTLESS HEART* was a three-masted carrack, its hull barnacle-crusted, its sails patched and repatched. It might once have been painted red, but the paint had long since faded and been scoured away by wind and water.

Donial, Alanya, and Kral watched its crew load cargo into its hold with ropes, pulleys, and nets. They had left Tarantia first thing in the morning, two days after breaking Kral out of jail, and ridden hard all that day. Conor had taken off on his own after the jailbreak, and they had not been able to find him in any of his usual haunts. Donial wished they had made him look into Alanya's mirror at some point, so they could have found him. Finally, they'd had to give up the search, as the Stygians were getting farther and farther away.

Now, in the dark of night, they stood wearily on the docks, observing the ship they hoped would take them down the Tybor. According to one of the dock-hands, it was the only ship that would be headed that way for the next several days. It carried cargo bound from the manufactories of Tarantia to points south, in Argos and beyond. The dockhand claimed that it also would carry another party from Tarantia, headed, like themselves, for Stygia.

The dockhand had described the ship's captain to them. They waited in the shadows, away from the flickering torches, until the man showed himself. Donial, cold, tired, and hungry, wished the fool would appear soon so they could settle things. They had covered a considerable distance today, with few stops, trying to catch up to the Stygians, who they knew had a substantial lead.

Finally, when Donial could barely keep his eyes open, Kral said, "That must be him." Donial, imme-diately alert, looked toward where Kral pointed. Sure enough, a man stood there looking at the ship with a proprietary air. He was a tall man, almost as tall as Conor but weighed probably half as much. He wore a wide-brimmed, floppy hat with a long feather stuck into it that made him look even taller, and a lit-tle ridiculous. In addition to that, he wore a long, dark blue coat over an open-chested white shirt, and pantaloons with a gold stripe down the sides, tucked into high boots. A red sash circled his waist, and a cutlass dangled from a chain there. He looked to Donial like someone who hoped to come off as a buccaneer and instead just appeared silly.

"Do we have to not laugh at him when we talk to him?" Alanya asked quietly.

"That would be best," Kral responded. "Come on, before he goes on board."

He stepped from the shadows, with Donial and Alanya close behind. They had agreed that Alanya would do the negotiating, since she was older than Donial, and Kral's appearance—not to mention his atrocious accent—might make things more difficult. So Donial gave Alanya a little push, forcing her out front.

She swatted at Donial's hand, but the captain had heard her shuffling footsteps and turned to face them. "Excuse me, are you Captain Ferrin?" she asked politely.

"Aye, missy, that's me," the captain said. He doffed his hat and swept it past his flat belly, in some kind of alternative to a bow. "What brings you to this neighborhood so late at night?" He raised an eyebrow at the appearance of the Pict behind her. In deference to the cool river air, Kral had draped a black cloak across his broad shoulders, but was otherwise typically bare-chested, wearing his usual loincloth and sandals. "And with such unusual company, no less."

"This is my brother Donial, and our friend Kral," Alanya explained. "We seek passage down the Tybor River to Stygia. Or as close to it as you'll go."

Captain Ferrin put his hat back on and stroked his narrow mustache. "A bold girl. I can appreciate that. And with a bold plan, to boot. Tell me, bold girl, can you pay for your passage?"

"Of course," Alanya affirmed. Cheveray had advanced them some gold, knowing that money would become an issue. "We would not ask it if we couldn't."

"So . . . passage for three, to Stygia. Hmm . . ." Ferrin made some quick mental calculations and named a price.

Donial could barely believe the figure he cited. "That's robbery!"

"Hush, Donial," Alanya said. She turned back to Ferrin. "He is right. That is far too much. We will pay half that."

Ferrin hesitated a moment, and in his eyes a new respect gleamed. "Split the difference and we can talk."

Alanya accepted the deal as Donial steamed. He didn't like being overruled in such a public and obvious fashion. He should have been accustomed to it, he knew—Alanya had been doing it since he was an infant. But it never failed to bother him. It was as if she did not care in the least what his opinion was.

In dealing with Ferrin, however, she must have

made the right decision. A little haggling was traditional, but arguing over price, especially with the insulting tone that Donial had first taken, might have made the captain lose interest altogether. As it was, he smiled charmingly, and said, "I have a previous arrangement with another party," he said. "But since you are willing to be accommodating, let me check to see if that party has any objection to the three of you booking passage at the same time. I shall return forthwith."

He turned and headed toward his ship. Alanya faced Donial and Kral with a smile on her face. "He looks absurd, but he seems nice enough," she said. "I am sorry I cut you off, Donial. I didn't think we should be rude. This is the only ship that has a chance of catching up to those Stygians. Missing it is out of the question."

"I understand," Donial said. He did, but he was unable to disguise his unhappiness over the way she had treated him.

"Alanya speaks the truth," Kral put in. "Not that the money is my own, but if we cannot make this ship, those priests will be so far ahead we would never find the Teeth."

"I know!" Donial snapped. He had already given in. He didn't need both of them ganging up on him. "I just thought we would want to save some of what we have until we get there. Who knows what we might face in Stygia, after all? And we have to get home, too."

"We will," Alanya assured him. "But right now, making progress is the most important thing."

Donial didn't answer, wanting just to let the argument drop. Instead of speaking, he pulled his heavy leather cloak tighter about himself and held it against the stiff breeze that blew in off the water. On the deck, he could see Captain Ferrin talking to a dark-haired man, nodding and gesturing back toward the three on the dock. After a couple of minutes of discussion, the other man went belowdecks, leaving Ferrin by himself, pacing and waiting. Donial turned away, not caring to watch any longer. He was tired. He wanted to get matters settled, one way or another, so he could get some sleep.

A few minutes later, Ferrin returned, walking as stiff-legged as a stork. He wore a huge smile on his skinny face. "I have good news," he said. "My other client has no objection to your presence on the *Restless Heart*."

"So you will take us?" Alanya asked with obvious excitement.

"I should be happy to," Ferrin said. "Payment in advance, of course."

"Half in advance, half on arrival," Alanya countered.

Ferrin laughed and bowed his head forward, hat on this time. "You are a skilled negotiator, lady," he said. "Welcome to my vessel."

• • •

AT FERRIN'S REQUEST, Gorian had gone be-lowdecks to the private cabin he had arranged with the lanky seaman. The rest of the mercenaries shared quarters with the ship's crew, except for a few who had been relegated to the cargo area. But Gorian needed privacy, and Kanilla Rey had been willing to pay a little extra to be sure he got it. Before they had even cast off, he would start to get his money's worth.

Around his neck he wore a leather thong, and at-tached to that thong, wrapped in a fine wire setting, was a small piece of plain gray rock. Kanilla Rey had said it was but a tiny piece of a larger stone that he kept in his *sanctum sanctorum.* When Gorian needed to contact him, he had only to cut his palm and press some blood into the rock, stare into it, and repeat some phrases that had been drummed into his head. He took the rock out and looked at it, then let it fall back against his chest while he sliced open his hand with a dagger. He could not remember any occasion on which Kanilla Rey had taught him the proper phrases, but he found that he knew them nonetheless. *"Ia nimtu kenata ia ia!"* he said, holding the rock in his bleeding hand. *"Quietus nictu camala Kanilla Rey."*

After a few seconds, he seemed to sense another presence nearby. The rock in his hand had turned clear. He could see his own palm through it. The other being he sensed in the cabin was invisible—present, but not seen. "Yes, Gorian?" a voice said.

The voice was Kanilla Rey's, though the man was miles away. "You called for me," Kanilla Rey's disembodied voice continued, when Gorian didn't answer immediately. "What is it?"

"The ship's captain, Ferrin," Gorian said quickly, not knowing how long the strange mystical conversation could last. "He says three young people are seeking passage on the ship with us. Their destination, like ours, is Stygia. They are willing to pay well, and he would like to let them come aboard."

Kanilla Rey's voice was quiet for a moment, and Gorian wondered if the sorcerous link with his employer had already been disrupted. But then the magician spoke again. "I see no problem. Make sure no one talks to them about your mission, and do not fraternize with them in any way."

"Of course," Gorian said. Both those things were understood.

"Very well," Kanilla Rey's voice said. "This is a difficult business, Gorian," he added. "Never use it unless it is absolutely necessary."

"Certainly," Gorian said. He expected some response, but the voice did not speak again, and the presence he had felt near him was no longer there.

In his bloody palm, the little sliver of rock was dull gray again.

He knew that there had been a time that he would have been terrified of something like the stone—of holding magic in the palm of his hand. Working it himself, by uttering those phrases. He was no wizard.

But he wasn't afraid now. He was becoming Kanilla Rey's creature, he guessed, accustomed to strange magics, accepting of whatever orders came his way.

Satisfied, he went topside to tell Captain Ferrin to let the young people board. He would keep an eye on them and make sure they didn't make any trouble for his men, or his mission.

ALANYA HAD EXPECTED that Captain Ferrin would launch his ship at first light. But once they had agreed on the terms and she had paid half the sum, he hurried them on board and showed them to the cabin they would share. It was cramped, but big enough for the three of them, with four bunks and a single filthy porthole. They tried to make themselves comfortable, all too exhausted to talk much. Donial fell asleep almost immediately, snoring softly. Kral's breathing was steady and even, and she thought he might be asleep as well. Alanya sat back in her bunk, beneath Kral's, and tried to imagine what might wait ahead for them.

But she found that she could not even envision what would come. Stygia was a strange and mysterious place, but in her imagination it was all towering sand dunes and dark sorceries, with images of snakes everywhere. She doubted that view was realistic, but knew not what else might be there. She couldn't quite believe they would have to battle a Stygian sorcerer for the crown.

At the same time, she knew that Kral would do so, if it became necessary. He had already demonstrated that he would not shy away from any task or any fight.

She clutched her magic mirror close to her—not that she expected it to be useful on this journey, but because, having been separated from it once, she refused to be again. She found herself wishing it could show the future, not just the past.

Within an hour, the ship's gentle rocking changed, and she knew that it had cast off, into the river's channel. The water flowed from here toward the sea, so the first leg would be the easiest part of the journey for the ship's crew.

Thinking about Captain Ferrin, she decided that she found him oddly charming. He laughed easily, and he strewed compliments about like sweets at a party. While he looked comical, she had noticed that he worked his crew efficiently yet without malice. Perhaps there was even fondness there, of captain for crew and vice versa. It had been a stroke of luck, the ship being at the dock, nearly ready to set off down the river, at the end of their headlong dash from Tarantia. Their horses had been boarded in a public stable, and they had made immediately for the dock.

And just in time. Stygia waited.

Stygia, and the crown.

10

USAM GRUNTED WITH satisfaction at the scene before him. A hundred fires burned in the night. More. In every direction he turned, he could see sparks shooting into the night sky. His nostrils burned with the tang of woodsmoke. By morning, the smoke would overhang the valley like the fog that often settled there.

He was not even concerned about the Aquilonians seeing the fires. If the civilized fools managed to figure out what they portended, they still wouldn't know when the Picts were coming or how many there would be.

There had never been such a unified force of Picts. And as he had hoped, the Elk Clan village had become the staging point for the upcoming attack.

Which meant that he had become the most important Pict ever.

One of them, anyway. Mara, his wife, kept telling him not to get carried away with himself, and he tried. But he had pulled off an incredible feat—with the help of whichever Aquilonian had stolen the Teeth of the Ice Bear, and Mang of the Bear Clan, who had gone from clan to clan persuading them to unite at the Elk Clan's village.

Not every clan was represented, but most were. Enough. When their combined force swept out of the forests and into the villages filled with soft, spoiled settlers and their families, the Aquilonians would realize what a mistake they had made by trying to move into Pictish country. The Picts had been docile too long, entering into truce negotiations with Aquilonia when they should have been swarming their villages, burning their people alive, collecting their heads. That was about to end, and the piles of skulls around Usam's camp would be replenished ere long.

Usam heard a noise behind him, and turned. It was Mara, an elk skin over her shoulders, clutched tight before her chest with one hand. Her hair, almost entirely gray now, hung unadorned on both sides of her broad face. She rarely smiled. She was not smiling now.

"Admiring your army?" she asked, her tone mocking.

"That is what they are, like it or not," he replied. "The first real Pictish army."

"But not *your* army," she pressed.

"Whose, then? Mang's? He has gone back to the Bear Clan village, or what's left of it. He knows we will force the Aquilonians to give back the Teeth. He is preparing himself to become the new Guardian. Klea continues Kral's work, making sure the wall of Koronaka does not grow fast enough to be an obstacle to our attack. Kral himself has not been heard from. I fear that he is dead. So whose army would it be?"

"Perhaps it is no one's army," Mara said. "Or it is everyone's. Every Pict's. You will truly know if it is yours when it's time to lead them into battle. If they follow and obey only you, then I suppose it is your army after all."

"Who else would they follow?" Usam wanted to know. There had never been such an army, so there was no familiar form for it to take. They would have to create it as they went, and he intended to mold it the way he wanted, like so much riverbank clay. "They gather in my valley, eat my meat, burn my trees for warmth."

"If you take responsibility for them, then you own them in failure as well as success," Mara warned.

"I do not expect failure," Usam countered. "We will find the Teeth and return it to the Bear Clan."

"And if you fail?"

"Then tragedy befalls the Pictish people, and anyone else in the way, with the Ice Bear's return. But before that happens, we'll take plenty of Aquilonians

to the Mountains of the Dead with us," Usam said.
"We may all die in the effort, but we will not die
alone."

ALONE IN HIS *sanctum sanctorum,* Kanilla Rey prepared for a monumental undertaking. He had fasted
for two days, sitting inside a room with three fire pits
burning, dripping water onto hot stones to generate
steam to sweat the impurities from his system. He
had chanted and prayed. He had meditated for hours
on end, until his muscles cramped.

He stood in a fresh purple robe, with clean gold
linens wrapped about his limbs, above a map that he
had unrolled on the floor. Using a piece of soft, pale
rock, he inscribed lines on the map, making a rectan-
gular shape just off the coast of Shem, which lay between the mouth of the Tybor River and Stygia. As he
drew, he muttered complex incantations learned from
a book called *The Forbidden Mysteries,* penned by
the long-dead wizard Xuatahul Divierus. He had pur-
chased the tome from a Nemedian vendor of rare
arcana, after long and strenuous negotiations that followed months of searching. The quest had resulted in
the deaths of three men, which Kanilla Rey felt was a
reasonable price to pay.

The initial incantations done, he turned to a pail
of water to which he had added certain ingredients.
With a ladle, he scooped out some of the liquid.

Speaking words over it in an ancient tongue, he splashed it on the map, in the area he had marked off. He turned to his right, made three complete circles, then splashed more of the water. The map curled and wrinkled under the dousing, but still he continued, first circling to the right again, then dripping more water, always muttering his spells.

As he did so, he felt a sudden weariness overtake him. He had not slept or eaten in days, so some degree of exhaustion was not unexpected. But the fatigue was much more than that. It was bone deep, utterly consuming, as if he had walked all the way to Stygia and back without a break for rest or nourishment. He could barely keep his eyes open.

No matter. It only meant that his spell had taken effect, he knew. Great works of magic drew energy from the magician and cast it into the world. He let the ladle sink into the pail and set the whole thing down on the stone floor, beside the map. He shook his head vigorously, flapped his hands and arms, trying to relax them, to stimulate the flow of blood through his extremities.

He was done. The Stygians sent by Shehkmi al Nasir to steal the strange Pictish crown out from under him would find that their voyage home would not be as easy as their surreptitious trip here had been. Kanilla Rey's agents had left considerably later than the Stygians, but that disadvantage would be minimized by this spell.

As he headed for his sleeping mat, Kanilla Rey smiled.

NONE OF THE Stygian acolytes had seen the storm coming. One minute they had been sailing clear seas, with bright stars twinkling overhead. The next, dark clouds roiled in the sky, blotting out those same stars. The wind that had filled their sails shifted suddenly, whipping canvas around, shearing lines, finally cracking the jib.

The sea, which had been calm, bucked and swelled beneath them. Standing on the deck, water stung their faces. As they dipped into a trough, the steering oars jerked from the hands of the men who had been holding them. The bow dropped, turning away from their course.

One of the acolytes who had been at the oars swore to Set. His oar continued to flop around too fast—if he were to grab it again, it would break his wrists, maybe even take his hands off altogether. "We are being blown off course!" he shouted.

"Correct it!" the third acolyte returned. The first could barely hear over the roar of the wind, the snap of the sails, and the thunder of the waves. *If it were that easy,* the oarsman thought angrily, *I would have done it already.* Shehkmi al Nasir had promised them an easy journey, with ensorcelled winds that would carry them along quickly and safely.

Something had gone very wrong with that plan. Cold water slashed at him like the strands of a whip. Ship's lines flew in the wind like a kraken's tentacles, wet and heavy. The acolyte was no sailor—none of them were. *Tend the steering oars,* Shehkmi al Nasir had said. *Keep the sails taut, and you will be fine.*

Instead, they were adrift in a sea that seemed determined to swallow the bireme whole. Had they sufficient oarsmen, they could still have rowed their way to shore, or to safer seas. But their master had determined that oarsmen would not be necessary, save one for steering. A wave crashed across the port gunwale, nearly swamping them, trying its best to drag them under. The acolyte swore again, and grabbed a line lest he be swept off the deck.

Cold, wet, discouraged, he shivered and bailed water uselessly with his free hand. It was turning into a very long night.

SHARING A SHIP with strangers was . . . well, strange, Alanya thought. The men who were the *Restless Heart*'s primary passengers were obviously mercenaries of some sort. But she didn't know where they were bound, or what they planned to do there, although her guess was that they were meant to fight someone, or worse. She had known men like them at Koronaka, and, though her brother had tried to befriend them, she had found her sensibilities disturbed by them. They were hard-looking men, raw at the edges, surly and tough. She heard them speaking among themselves from time to time, usually in Aquilonian, but she never caught enough to discern their mission. They never spoke directly to her, or to Kral or Donial, except to acknowledge them if they passed in the passageway or on deck.

Well, they did not know what she and her companions were up to either. They shared a hull that kept them dry and safe, and sails and oars that had sped them down the Tybor, passing barges and fishing craft and other, slower vessels, in only four days' time. The same trip, on horseback, would have taken many more. But the winds were with them, Captain Ferrin said, as was the current.

And, just possibly, the captain had added with a rakish grin, the gods. A speedier journey he had never known.

Alanya wasn't sure she believed that, but she would not have been surprised if the ship had assistance from some unnatural source. It moved with a speed and agility that seemed suspect to her, cutting through the water like a great serpent. Its sails were always full, its oarsmen always strong. A drummer kept a steady beat going, and the oars, eighteen on each side, dipped into the river, drew, and rose, to his rhythm.

Alanya did not know who, or what, had interceded on their behalf, if indeed there was any intercession at all. Nor did she care. She only knew that speed served her purpose, so she was not inclined to question it.

The sooner they reached Stygia—or caught up with the Stygians on their own voyage home—the sooner Kral could get his crown back. Then she and Donial could return to Tarantia to stay. She was the mistress of a house now, an estate, and she needed to be there. Cheveray had agreed to run their father's business interests during their absence, but he could not be expected to do so forever. Besides, she still had not even had a chance to tell her friends that she was alive.

She stood at the ship's bow, watching the seas ahead, almost glassy in the morning sun. She wished Conor had come with them on this quest instead of disappearing. She blamed Donial for that. His idea had been sound, but settling for the first muscular fellow they had run across, instead of taking the time to choose one who would be loyal and responsible, had been a mistake. As soon as they had paid him a little something, he had vanished. So they were on their own again, following a faint trail, hoping against hope that they would be able to find the missing crown. And able to take it away from those who had it.

"I have never seen so much water."

The voice startled her, and she spun around. It was only Kral, though, having come up behind her with his quiet Pictish tread. He smiled at her discomfort.

"Sorry," he said. "I did not mean to startle you. It's just . . . I am not used to traveling on a ship."

"I know," she said. "I'm not either. But we make much better time than we would have on land."

"Yes," Kral agreed, nodding.

"Do you think this will work, Kral?" she asked. She had been gripped by a sudden bout of despair. "Do you think we can find the crown? What if it is already in Stygia? It's such a tiny thing, in such a huge place."

Kral shrugged and furrowed his brow. "I know not," he admitted. "I hope that we can. If Stygian priests did indeed steal it, as Conor reports, they must have some reason for wanting it. I think that reason, whatever it may be, will be what leads us to it. If you and Donial wish to return—"

Alanya cut him off midsentence. "Kral, you know better than that. We are here. We are in this with you. However long it takes. Yes, I would rather be in Tarantia than on this ship. But only once you also have what you seek, as I do." What she left unsaid was the knowledge that once he had the crown, he would return to the Pictish wilderness with it, back to his savage ways, full of undeniable hardship and casual cruelty. When they had successfully completed their journey, he would be gone from her life, probably forever. Powerful and handsome, feet widely spaced to brace him against the rocking motion—even as out of place as on the deck of a sailing ship heading out to sea, he was a source of strength to her, an inspiration.

A friend.

Maybe, someday, more than that.

But only if she could keep him close.

"I know, Alanya," he said. "I only meant—"

Again, his sentence was interrupted.

But this time, not by her.

11

"CLEAR THE DECK! Get below, you lot!"

It was Captain Ferrin, shouting at them and gesticulating wildly. Alanya had to grab the railing, because the ship lurched suddenly. Cold spray drenched her and Kral, who reached for Alanya to steady her. She was nearer the rail than he was, and he didn't want to lose her overboard.

"Captain, what is . . . ?" she began.

"It's a squall!" he answered tersely. "Came up from nowhere. Get below, now. It's going to be a bad one!"

Kral looked at the sky, steel gray and glowering, and at the rain that had begun to sheet down on them, as if some malicious god emptied enormous buckets.

Even the waves had changed. The peaks grew white and choppy, and the gulfs deep and dark. Captain Ferrin had already turned away from them and shouted orders to the crew, demanding that the sails be struck immediately, lest they be torn or the masts broken. "He's right," Kral said to Alanya. "Come on."

Her grip on the rail was fast, white-knuckled. But he took her other hand and she released the railing, moving unsteadily toward him. "Kral, this is not . . . this cannot be natural."

He was inclined to agree. The sea had been calm just moments before. There had been no indication of a storm, no warning. But he was not familiar with the sea. Maybe it happened all the time.

That seemed unlikely, though.

He helped Alanya to the hatchway and down the ladder. Their cabin was belowdecks, and Donial had been inside, brooding in his bunk, a little seasick, when Kral had gone up looking for Alanya.

If the boy had been seasick before, he would be truly unhappy under these circumstances, Kral supposed. He was feeling a little queasy himself.

When they reached the cabin, Donial's head was out the porthole. He heard them enter and glanced at them, his skin ashen, his hair soaked and plastered to his wet face. "I'm sick," he moaned.

"No shame in that," Kral told him. "Seas like this will do it to anyone." He didn't know that for sure, but he guessed it was probably true. And if it could make Donial feel better about his condition, it was a harmless lie.

Alanya crossed to her brother and stroked his back while he leaned out again. Water splashed in through the port, but Alanya paid it no mind. "The captain says we have hit a sudden squall," she explained. "I doubt it will stay like this for very long."

"It's already too long for me," Donial said, bringing his head inside again. He shut the porthole. "I'm empty."

One small blessing, Kral thought. "Alanya's right," he said. "This cannot last very long. And I heard a sailor say that if it looks like it will, the ship will make for shore and tie down until it passes."

"Which would cost us valuable time," Alanya observed.

"Perhaps. But in this storm, we run the risk of losing ground instead of gaining. Better to play it safe than capsize out here." The ship wasn't running very far out anyway—just away from hidden reefs and shallow water, but Captain Ferrin had said the coastline would be visible for the whole trip to Stygia. "So the others, the mercenaries, they are also headed for Stygia?" Kral had asked the captain.

Ferrin had ignored the question. Which answered it, as far as Kral was concerned. Answered it in the affirmative.

Why a crew of mercenaries would be going to Stygia, he had no idea.

But they bore watching, just the same. He had done his best to keep an eye on them since the voyage began.

A wave crashed against the ship, shoving it to starboard with such force that Alanya's feet went out from under her. She crashed into Donial, who still stood by the bulkhead. Even Kral lost his balance, dropping to hands and knees on the deck. The ship righted, then rocked to port, but less violently.

"That was bad," Donial said, when his sister had disentangled herself.

"Yes," Kral agreed. "We are best off in our bunks, I think. And holding on to something."

He took his own suggestion, and the others followed suit. They could hear water pounding against the hull. The ship pitched and yawed sickeningly. It felt to Kral like being inside a cloud during the worst kind of thunderstorm. In their bunks, at least they were dry, and they could clutch the bunk poles to keep them from being thrown about. Occasionally, when the wind died momentarily, or the ship caught on the crest of a wave, they could hear furious shouts and running feet out on the deck. The oarsmen's drummer was hard at work, picking out a fast and steady rhythm. Kral doubted that the oars were helping much, although with the sails struck, they were all that propelled the ship besides the waves themselves.

Part of him wanted to go topside and watch the sailors battle the storm. It would be dramatic, he knew. He pictured them, rain-lashed, windblown, tugging on lines and pulling on oars, fighting nature with every ounce of their strength, as a Pict would fight an enemy. Their faces would be set, jaws firm, teeth clenched. The muscles would stand out on their arms, corded with steely sinew, as they worked.

But he thought his presence in the cabin soothed Alanya. And on deck, he might be in the way. He didn't know a jib sail from a mizzenmast, and he would hate to become an obstacle instead of a help.

So he stayed where he was, trying to ignore the continuous thunder of water assaulting the ship and the uncertain lurching of its progress. After what seemed like an hour, he risked going to the porthole to look out. The incessant rain was almost impenetrable, but he was sure he could see land, not far away.

"We're almost to shore," he told the others. "The captain's probably just looking for a sheltered spot to anchor."

"Let's hope so," Donial answered weakly. "I don't know how much more of this I can stand."

"It will not be long now," Kral declared. Sheer speculation, but he hoped it was true. "I am certain of it."

ON DECK, CAPTAIN Ferrin could scarcely believe the luck. He had made this journey many times, ferrying goods and occasional passengers between the desert kingdom of Stygia and the civilized one of Aquilonia. He knew every inch of the coastline, having sailed it in good seas and in bad.

But never had he encountered a storm like this one, so swift in its attack, so fierce in its determination to sink his ship. The wind seemed to change direction every minute, so that he never knew from where it would blow next. The waves were like living, malevolent beings, picking the absolute worst moments to push up beneath the *Restless Heart*'s hull, then to fall away, dropping her twenty feet or more to slam against their hard surface below. The deck was flooded; he stood knee deep in cold, swirling water.

His oarsmen did their best, and in this one instance the storm seemed to cooperate, pushing them unceasingly toward the shore. That was where he wanted to be. There was a protected inlet, he was positive, not far from here. He couldn't see it through wind and water, but he knew it well. If he could coax the *Heart* in there, he could save her.

It was not to be, though. When he heard the splintering of wood, he realized it was too late for that. They wouldn't make the inlet or any other destination. A wave lifted the ship off whatever they'd struck, and he was grateful for that. But the tilt of the deck, the sight of water running off it to port, told him the damage had already been done.

"We've run aground!" he screamed. "Hole in the port side, astern! Man the boats! Prepare to abandon ship!"

The *Restless Heart* carried a crew of forty sailors. Twenty-three passengers, among both groups, and himself, made sixty-four.

There was space on the lifeboats for thirty.

They weren't too far from shore. Most could swim it. At least, in normal seas, they could have.

In these seas, it was anyone's guess how many would make it alive.

"ABANDON SHIP?" ALANYA echoed. "That sounds bad."

"Hush," Kral urged. He opened the porthole a crack so he could hear better. Even as he did, he knew from the listing of the ship that Alanya had heard correctly. He could tell that she was terrified. Much as he didn't like to admit it, he, too, felt dizzy—from the chaotic motion of the ship, and from the fear rising inside him. All this effort, all this distance, just to have a seemingly solid vessel fall apart beneath their feet, dumping them into the ocean's trackless depths? "Yes," he said. "It's time to go."

"But . . . does this ship have boats?" Donial asked. "Or must we swim for it?"

Kral pointed to port, or north, from there. "Land is

not too far that way," he said. "If we have to swim, we stay together. If the ship breaks up, there will be wood we can use to help us float."

"You're serious," Alanya said, incredulous. "Swimming to shore? Where are we?"

"That must be Shem over there," Donial said. "Where in Shem, I have no idea."

"I have never been to Shem," Alanya admitted. She tried to put on a brave front, Kral knew, but her voice trembled, as did her hand when she scooped up her mirror and tucked it into a pouch hidden under her skirts. "Or wanted to. But it looks like we will end up there anyway."

"Better that than staying on this while it sinks," Kral agreed. "Let's go."

He helped them to the ladder, then up and onto the deck. Captain Ferrin was busy supervising the launching of lifeboats—only two of them, Kral noted, and too small to carry more than a fraction of those on board. Ferrin's floppy hat was gone, his long dark hair glued to his head. If he looked as ridiculously stiltlike as ever, he also looked like a man who knew what he was doing. He barked orders with authority, and his gaze swept the deck, keeping an eye on changing conditions at all times. Spotting Alanya and Donial on deck, he gestured them over.

"Them first!" he commanded. "The girl and the boy!"

"We need not—" Alanya began.

Her brother interrupted her. "It is tradition," he said. "Women and children first. I am no child, and I'll take my own chances. But you need to get on that boat, or no one else will."

Kral could tell that she was hesitant, not wanting to be separated from Donial or him. He did not want her separated either, but he knew that Donial was right. The sailors would put her on the first boat if they had to pick her up and throw her on board.

"You are no child," he whispered to Donial. "But take advantage of the chance to go with her. She might need you."

Donial frowned at him. "But I—"

"No one is calling you a little boy," Kral said. "But you are the youngest on board. If they want to consider you a child for this purpose, then it is to our benefit. We do not want to leave Alanya alone with them."

"Very well," Donial said. "She is my sister, after all. I will look after her." His acceptance was grudging, but he took Alanya's hand, and together they went to the boat, which had already splashed down into the sea and was crashing against the ship's hull with every wave.

As surely as he knew getting Donial on the lifeboat had been the right thing to do, Kral knew that he would never get on it. He was nothing but a savage to these people. Little better than an animal. He would be the absolute last person allowed on a boat, and it was already clear that there were not enough spaces for everyone. Sailors lowered Alanya and Donial to the little rowboat, then took their own places on it, breaking out oars and pushing away from the *Restless Heart*. The next boat filled up fast as well, mostly with the mercenaries who were Captain Ferrin's paying passengers.

When both boats had pushed off and struck for shore, the remaining sailors waited for Captain Ferrin's order. Once given, they dove into the churning sea and began to swim.

And then there were only two on the swamped deck. Kral, and the captain. "What are you waiting for, lad?" Ferrin demanded. "Swim for it."

"What about you?" Kral asked.

"There is a maritime custom," Captain Ferrin replied, "that the captain goes down with his ship."

"That sounds stupid," Kral noted.

"It is," Ferrin said. "Like some other customs I could name. And like those, it is really a matter of personal choice. I have only waited this long to be sure everyone else got away safely. You included, Pict. So get into the water, because I cannot until you do!"

The captain might have looked absurd, but his stock rose in Kral's estimation when he spoke. With no reason to tarry, Kral sucked in a huge breath, held it, and dove into the sea. He swam beneath the surface until he could stand it no longer, then came out and gasped for air.

As soon as his head broke the water, he saw the captain's splash, close behind. Together, matching stroke for stroke, they made for the shore.

12

THE LITTLE BOAT was no great improvement over drowning, as far as Donial was concerned.

The waves sloshed into it at will, leaving the people inside soaked, bailing for their lives with pails, helmets, and hands. Tossed by the waves, the boat bucked and bounced even more than the ship had. Donial was sick again, and this time he wasn't alone. Even seasoned sailors were green-faced and retching.

Enough remained unaffected to row the boat, however. They pulled for the shore, invisible through the downpour except as a low, dark mass in the distance. Alanya gripped his hand so hard it hurt, but he was glad for the contact.

After a while, the combination of terror, water, cold, and the inability to see beyond the confines of the small craft started to get to him, and he felt drowsy. It would be easy, he thought, to drift off to sleep. So easy . . .

He shook himself awake, even going so far as to pinch his own leg. Sleeping now was not an option, he realized. Too much likelihood that he would fall right out of the boat, possibly even dragging his sister along. He had to stay alert, no matter what.

Realizing that Alanya was staring at him, he offered her what he hoped was an encouraging smile. "It will not be long now," he said.

"I hope not."

In the next few minutes, Donial began to take heart himself. The sea seemed marginally more calm. The waves pushed the boat in only one direction—the same way the oarsmen rowed—instead of toward what seemed like every compass point at once. The shoreline came into sharper relief.

Since Donial had been hoisted into the boat, he had not seen Kral. A few times, he had caught glimpses of the second lifeboat, not too far behind his. But he had no idea if the Pict was in that boat or somewhere out at sea.

More minutes passed, during which the shore became clearly delineated. Waves crashed against a series of boulders jutting up from the surface. Beyond those, the water was calm. It lapped against a sandy beach that angled up toward what looked like a vast stretch of unbroken grassland. Donial had half expected ziggurats rising whitely from the land, or desert chieftains on camelback grinning at the shipwreck survivors with sharp scimitars in their hands. But there were no buildings here, no towns in sight, or people of any description. Just empty coast as far as he could see. A white stretch of sand, then grass—not desert, after all—beyond.

Then they were there. Sailors jumped from the boat and splashed ashore, grabbing its gunwales and dragging it through a break in the boulders and onto the beach. Rain continued to patter down around them, but they had made landfall, dry or not.

As soon as the craft was beached, Donial jumped out, then extended a hand to help Alanya. She climbed out of the boat and stood there in the surf. Waves washed up to her knees as she stared out at the dark sea.

Looking for Kral, Donial knew.

Looking for the one who was the reason they were here in the first place. Shipwrecked, maybe marooned in the middle of nowhere.

And still, to her, the most important person in the world.

Donial mentally cursed himself for thinking that, as soon as he did. He knew that he was Alanya's first priority, as she was his. They were family, and nothing could ever change that.

Of course, a niggling thought at the back of his mind reminded him, Uncle Lupinius and Father were siblings, too. And look what had happened there. He still did not know, of course, if Lupinius had actually killed his father. But Lupinius had watched it happen, by his own admission. And if it hadn't happened exactly as he had described—which seemed very unlikely—then he was still guilty. It had been his idea, after all, to attack the Pictish village, using Kral as an excuse.

Nothing like that could ever happen between him and Alanya, though. They argued sometimes, they resented one another—that was natural, and he was sure it was the same with all siblings. And now that they had business interests together—now that they would have to run their father's estate—it was entirely possible that they would clash more, rather than less. But mostly, they loved and watched out for each other. For his part, he would rather have stayed home in Tarantia than gone on this foolhardy expedition, chasing around the world looking for the Pictish crown. Alanya, however, would not have stayed behind, so here Donial was, too.

Family did that for family.

THERE WERE MOMENTS when Kral thought he might not make it.

The waves never let up, never stopped fighting him. He pulled and pulled until it felt like his arms would tear off at the shoulders. His lungs ached. He had swallowed so much foul, salty seawater he thought he would sink. Every time he brought his head above the surface there was so much rain and spray he could barely tell if he was above water or not. And the waves bashed and threw him around so much he was afraid he had lost track of which direction he was supposed to be swimming.

But giving up was not the Pictish way. He redoubled his efforts, pawing at the water with cupped hands, kicking with powerful legs. He sliced through the waves like a sharp knife through the tender flesh of a young deer.

Soon enough, he saw results. The distant coastline swam into focus, and shortly after that he could even see the boats up on the shore. They had made it, he thought with satisfaction. Alanya and Donial were safe. The knowledge gave him renewed strength.

Sometime later, he gained the beach and stumbled onto the sand, exhausted. He heard his name called, assumed that it was Alanya, but collapsed facedown onto the wet ground anyway. He felt hands on his back, his ribs, turning him over. He blinked seawater from his eyes, looked up, and started to laugh.

"Kral?" Alanya said, concerned. "What are you laughing at? What is so amusing?"

Kral managed to control himself long enough to answer. Alanya was still as beautiful as always, despite the fact that her golden hair was matted to her skull, caked with sand, and tangled with seaweed, her face was crusted with salt, and her clothing was soaked and shredded. "When I first saw you I thought you were a goddess," he said, allowing himself another chuckle. "And perhaps you are. But now, I think probably a goddess of the sea."

She regarded him for a long moment—probably trying, he guessed, to determine if he had been knocked on the head or swallowed so much seawater that he had gone mad. But then she smiled, too, and started to laugh along with him. "I imagine I am a sight," she said. "But then, you look no better yourself right now."

"You are probably right," Kral said. He knew she had the mirror with her; knew, also, that she would not want to reveal it to the men around them. "I started out less lovely than you, though."

Alanya laughed again, and punched him playfully on the arm. "Maybe you should have just drowned," she said teasingly. Then, as if realizing what she had said, she threw her arms about him and embraced him tightly. "I did not mean that!"

He held her close, and would have been willing to go on holding her as long as he could. Even if she had meant it, he wouldn't have cared, as long as he got to embrace her.

CAPTAIN FERRIN PACED back and forth on the beach. The storm had finally blown over. Late-afternoon sunlight slanted beneath the retreating clouds. He could see the *Restless Heart* offshore, run aground on the same reef that had first torn a hole in her. She listed to port, but hadn't sunk or broken up. Which meant, he guessed, that the damage had not been as bad as he had feared.

Both boats had made it to shore, and a head count revealed that only seven had been lost swimming. Four had been mercenaries, three his own crew. The Pict who had waited with him had made it to the beach several minutes before him.

So, all things considered, things were not as bad as they might have been. It was even possible that the ship could be repaired. There were a few trees around, tall, skinny palms, that they could use for wood if need be. In the grasslands there were probably rabbits, maybe even deer, on which they could survive while they worked on her. And there were always fish, of course.

All he had to do was make the decision. Strike out overland, on foot, in which case they could be in Argos within a week, probably, two at the outside? Or stay put and try to fix the ship—knowing that if he judged wrong, and she was beyond repair, he would only have delayed the inevitable overland trek?

If they retreated to Argos, he knew his passengers would demand their fares back. And he would have lost his cargo—much of which was no doubt already waterlogged and ruined. In the end, it was the financial considerations that made his mind up for him.

"We're fixing her!" he shouted to his companions.

"Fixing the *Restless Heart*?" his first mate, an Ophirean named Allatin, asked.

"Aye," Ferrin replied. He stood with hands on his hips, grinning madly. "She's still seaworthy, I warrant. Look at her there, even now."

Gorian, the man who had arranged passage for the mercenaries, approached Ferrin, scowling darkly. "Can it be done quickly, Captain?" he asked quietly. "Our business is urgent, and we can brook no delays."

"We are delayed already, man," Ferrin answered. "It will take what it takes, no more or less. We'll get to work as fast as we can—it is too late for today, but on the morrow. If your men will pitch in, the work will go that much faster."

"These are fighting men, not shipwrights," Gorian said. "But they will pitch in where they can."

"Good," Ferrin said. "The more hands, the better. Don't worry, I will tell them what to do."

"You tell me," Gorian said. "I tell them. They take no orders from you, or any other."

"As you like," Ferrin replied, in no mood to argue the point. More workers were better than fewer, even if he had to work through another man.

At least Gorian wasn't asking for his gold coins back yet. Maybe, thought Ferrin, he knew the gold was still on the ship.

• • •

ALANYA SAT WITH her back leaning against one of the palm trees that flanked the beach and her feet in the sand, enjoying the warm glow of the morning sun. The afternoon before, the sun had dried her off, and just in time, for it had sunk rapidly, and the night had been cool. She, Kral, and Donial had dug a furrow in the sand and curled up in it, with her in the middle, for warmth. She had been glad that the men would be making a trip out to the ship in the morning, hoping that in addition to examining the damage, they would bring back more dry clothes, and blankets, with them.

Now that it was morning, Kral had gone scouting and come back with freshwater contained in a skin that had washed ashore. She had known she was thirsty, but hadn't realized just how much she was craving water. She drank deeply, then he and Donial and some of the other men went back to the stream he had found to fetch more. They returned carrying it in hats, cups, clothing, and anything else they could.

Captain Ferrin drank his fill, then stalked the beach watching the rest. "We're wasting time," he barked. "Those of us who are going out, get to the boats!"

"I should go with them," Kral said quietly.

"No, stay here," Alanya pleaded. She had been afraid of losing him the day before and didn't want him out of her sight. "There are plenty of them."

"They will need as many men as they can get," Kral insisted.

"You know nothing about boats" she said. "Stay."

"Alanya, I need to go."

"Umm . . . Alanya . . ." Donial interrupted. "Kral. Who do you suppose *that* is?"

Alanya stood and looked off to the east, the direction in which her brother was staring and pointing.

In the far distance, across miles and miles of empty grasslands, she could see a line of people, looking tiny and antlike from there. They were too far away to make out any detail at all, but it was obvious that they were humans.

The other thing that was obvious, from the swath they cut through the grass, was that they were headed right for the survivors of the *Restless Heart*!

13

"CAPTAIN FERRIN!" KRAL called, after staring at the line of men for a few moments. "Look!"

The captain rushed up the beach to their vantage point among the palms, followed by a few of his men. "What is it?" he demanded, sounding angry that his immediate goal had been delayed.

"I do not know," Kral said truthfully. "But they come this way."

"He's right, Captain," said Allatin, the first mate. "Look at 'em all."

"Who do you think they are?" another sailor asked.

"A Shemish trading caravan, no doubt," Captain Ferrin said, after a brief hesitation. "Riding camels, I expect. They probably think we have goods to trade with them."

"If we could unload some of our cargo here . . ." Allatin mused. He was a wiry man, with lean, chiseled muscles and a long blond beard.

"We won't get a decent price from this lot," Ferrin argued. "Not under these conditions. If it will make them happy—especially if we can acquire any tools or materials to help us fix the *Restless Heart*—then we can part with a few barrels of wine, some silks, even some skins, if they have interest in those. But my customers in Stygia are expecting this shipment, and I'll deliver it to them on my back before I let these Shemites trade me their copper baubles for it."

"Maybe we could swap some of your Corinthian wine for their Kyros wine," one of the mercenaries suggested. "I've had but a single cup of it in my time, but I remember it as the sweetest I've ever tasted."

"You will note that the Corinthian wine is in the cargo hold," Ferrin reminded him. Kral observed that the lanky captain's hand had strayed, almost casually, to the hilt of his cutlass. "And that you are served mead, not wine, at your meals. My cargo is not for crew or passengers to consume."

The mercenary grumbled and spat into the sand, but he didn't press the issue. Maybe they thought the shipwreck would change things, Kral guessed. But Ferrin was still the captain, on dry land or at sea, and no man seemed interested in challenging that authority.

Kral drifted back to where Alanya and Donial stood, watching the caravan's progress. The black line came on, slowly but steadily. Kral's keen eyesight picked out more detail as they approached. "It looks to be about eighty men," he said quietly. "Walking, not mounted."

"Captain Ferrin said they would be on camels," Alanya commented.

"That makes no sense," Donial put in. "In the deserts of eastern Shem, sure. As in Stygia, it's all sand there, I understand. But in grass like this, I would expect horses, not camels."

"Me, too," Kral agreed. "But traders on foot? How would they carry their goods?"

"Maybe they are not traders, then," Alanya suggested.

"If not traders, who?" That, Kral knew, was the real question that needed to be answered. Whoever they were, they outnumbered the survivors of the *Restless Heart,* and most of the crew and mercenaries had left their weapons behind when they abandoned the ship. He felt more naked without his knife than without a loincloth, so he had brought his along. But Donial and Alanya were unarmed, as were many of the others. If those approaching had sinister designs, it would be a hard fight to win.

Leaving his friends again, he went to Captain

Ferrin and explained his concerns. The captain listened thoughtfully, peering across the distance at the oncoming force. He had done much to earn Kral's respect, and he didn't disappoint now. "Right you are, lad," he said when Kral had finished. "I don't think they are Shemish soldiers—they would be as likely to be mounted as traders, right? But now you mention it, if they were traders, they would have wagons to haul their goods, as well as mounts. This lot has none of that." He turned and sought out his first mate. "Allatin!" he called, seeing the fellow down by the beach.

When the mate had run to the captain's side, Ferrin said, "Get one of the boats and ferry a few men out to the *Heart*. Fast but quiet. Get on board, and fetch as many weapons as you can. Bows, arrows, a few spears wouldn't be a bad idea, but mostly close combat ones: swords, knives, axes. Some of those mercenaries carried pikes, bills, and maces—bring those as well. I know not who those men are or what they want, but I do not want us standing here with nothing in our hands but sand and palm fronds when they arrive."

"Aye," Allatin acknowledged. With brisk efficiency, he dashed down the beach and gathered half a dozen able seamen, and together they ran the lifeboat out into the surf.

"Good thinking, lad," Ferrin said, with a gracious smile for Kral. "If the love of the sea ever strikes you like it does other men, there will always be a place for you on my crew."

"Thank you, Captain," Kral replied. "I think I am happiest on solid ground, though." He glanced around at the flat, grassy meadow that extended away from there, as far as the eye could see. "With more trees around than this."

"Each to his own," Ferrin said. "But the offer stands."

Kral returned to Donial and Alanya. "He has sent men to the ship to gather weapons," he told them.

"Weapons?" Alanya asked. "Wouldn't we be better off with food? And maybe a few barrels of water?"

"There is food and water here," Kral countered. "But empty-handed, we may not live long enough to need it."

Without pausing or diverging from their course, the line of men continued to cut a swath through the grass, straight toward them. Gradually, they came close enough for Kral to see individuals with more clarity. Kral had never seen a Shemite, as far as he knew, but from what Alanya and Donial told him, the men who approached didn't look like them. Western Shemites, he was told, were big men with dark hair that shone almost blue in the midday sun. They would be wearing shirts of mail and would have conical steel helmets on their heads, and they would carry powerful bows with which they were as comfortable as with their own hands.

These men were nothing like Shemites. Kral saw a few with wide-brimmed hats like the one Captain Ferrin had lost, and others—like some of the sailors from the *Restless Heart*—with bandannas tied around their scalps. He saw gold glinting at their ears, around their necks, and at their wrists. He saw open shirts, wide belts, pantaloons tucked into knee-high, cuffed boots. And in their hands or at their sides, he saw cutlasses, and some crossbows. Weapons such as could be used on the decks of a ship, without entangling the lines.

"They're seamen!" he shouted when all this was clear to him. He knew that his vision was sharper than that of his more civilized companions. "Those are no meadow-dwellers or desert traders!"

Captain Ferrin heard him and rushed to his side. "If only I had not left my glass on the ship," he said. "But I will trust your barbaric eyesight over my own. Sailors, eh?"

"Yes, Captain, I am sure of it. They could be your crew, except that most of them are shorter and heavier than your men. Not a one of them is as tall as Allatin, much less your height."

"Short, you say." Kral noted an edge to the captain's voice that hadn't been there before. He swiveled around and looked toward the ship, which the men on the lifeboat had just reached. "Hurry, you lot," he said under his breath.

"Who do you think they are?" Kral asked.

"Well, they are not Shemites. From your description, I would guess maybe Argosseans. Which, to be on the safe side, we have to assume means Argossean pirates."

"Pirates?" Alanya echoed.

"The Baracha Islands are infested with them, like rats swarming a ship's hold," Ferrin explained. "They ply the coast between there and Kush, looking for easy prey. I've run up against them a time or two, but always escaped with my skin."

"Why would they be on land, in Shem?" Alanya asked.

"Same as we are, most likely," Kral answered. "We have no idea how long that storm had been raging, or where it was before it hit us. But it might have driven their ship aground, somewhere up ahead of us. If they were shipwrecked, they might be trying to reach Argos on foot."

"Aye, and we happen to be between them and their goal," Ferrin added. "With a ship that's still seaworthy, given a few repairs." He glanced at the *Restless Heart* again. The men were just then clambering aboard.

The next few minutes dragged out excruciatingly slowly for Kral. The group of men coming toward them compressed, so that instead of a spread-out line, they were almost in a phalanx formation. Having done so, they advanced more rapidly. Soon Kral could make out individual facial characteristics and expressions. The man at the front of the pack, for example, had a sneer on his face, a fresh gash across his left eyebrow and cheek, and his deep chest moved heavily beneath a shirt that had been torn almost to ribbons. Behind him were a number of men who all looked as though they'd fought to the gates of hell and back again.

At the ship, Kral saw the men who had been sent after weapons emerge from belowdecks, carrying arm-loads of them toward the lifeboat. One of them must have noticed how close the Argosseans had drawn, because he shouted out something to his fellows, and they all began to run with their loads.

Turning back to the Argosseans, Kral saw that they were now running, too. "To arms!" Captain Ferrin shouted—redundantly, as every sailor and merce-nary who had a weapon had long since drawn it.

Which still left more than half of them empty-handed.

Kral could hear their voices raised in throaty war cries, the thunder of boots on the dirt, the clink of steel on steel. He wished that he was painted for bat-tle, but there was nothing to paint with, not even good rich mud. He would just have to do without.

"Get behind me," he said to Alanya and Donial.

"Just get me a sword!" Donial complained. "I can fight."

"The swords will not be here in time," Kral replied. "Stay back!"

"Come, Donial," Alanya urged. She tugged him back behind the first line of defenders.

Kral was glad for the company of the mercenaries. There weren't enough of them, and most had been so quick to abandon the sinking ship that they had left their weapons behind. But at least they were used to fighting on land. The young Pict worried that the sailors' main battle experience was on ships, which doubtless required different skills.

The mercenaries—even those who were bare-handed, who had at least scooped up stones they could throw—joined the armed sailors in making a defensive arc around the rest of the group. The sailors on the lifeboat were rowing like mad for the shore, and one even stood up with a crossbow in his hands. But they were too far away to help.

Because the Argosseans were upon them. A series of crossbow bolts flew into the defenders' ranks, taking down two of them before the hand-to-hand fighting even started. Others snatched up the weapons of the fallen, closing ranks around their bodies.

The attackers charged in, swords flashing. Captain Ferrin was the first to meet a foe in combat, his cutlass clashing against that of one of the buccaneers so hard that sparks flew. Then Kral paid attention only to his own survival—a short, round barrel of a man, gap-toothed mouth open in a silent scream, came right for him, swinging a sinister curved sword. Kral ducked underneath that first swipe and jabbed up with his knife. But the man had a second blade, a short dagger, in his left hand, and he blocked Kral's attack with it. At the same moment he brought the cutlass whistling around toward Kral's neck and shoulder. Kral dodged to his left and the man's blade slammed into the earth. Rising from his crouch, Kral kicked the side of the blade so hard it wrenched the sword from the man's grip. His face took on a pan-icked expression as Kral moved into him, chest to chest, using his right hand to hold the other's left wrist and with his left, driving the knife into the man's meaty gut.

Kral released him with a shove backward, to keep him out of the line of defense. The man fell, choking and clawing at his own belly. A quick assessment told Kral that the line had held, so far. He couldn't see Captain Ferrin, but most of the other mercenaries and sailors still stood, and more of them were armed now, having taken weapons from their fallen foes—or from those of their comrades who had already died.

But the Argosseans kept coming, in such numbers that they were beginning to circle around the defen-sive arc. Kral knew that when they had to watch their backs as well as their fronts, the fight would end quickly. He snatched up the fallen pirate's cutlass and—noting Donial's anxious glare—tossed it in-stead to the nearest unarmed mercenary. The man gave a shout of thanks and hurried to the near end of the arc.

"Kral!" Alanya shouted urgently. He turned back to face the pirates, and two of them rushed at him with slashing swords and wicked grins on their faces. He wished for a moment that he'd kept the cutlass, but then he had no more time for wishing.

14

ALANYA WATCHED IN horror as Kral turned to face two attacking buccaneers. He let out a guttural cry and twisted his body so that one of the swords passed completely by him. The other one raked across his chest, though. Alanya saw blood fly in the air. She screamed.

Kral barely seemed to notice the wound, however. His knife was in his right hand, and he swung it at the pirate who had cut him, while with his left he caught the shoulder of the one who had missed. Forcing down on the shoulder, he pushed that man toward the ground. His knife stabbed the other in the upper arm, and once it had penetrated flesh and muscle Kral yanked it toward himself. The man gave out a howl of pain and hurled himself away from Kral, dropping the sword.

The other man started to pick himself up off the ground. Kral lashed out with one foot, catching the man just beneath the chin. The pirate spun around and collapsed into the grass.

Before she could stop him, Donial lunged away from her, grabbing one of the dropped swords. Kral caught the other one and handed it off to a waiting sailor. Her heart pounded as her little brother tried to maneuver his way into position to join the fighting. Kral blocked Donial's way as he did battle with another pirate; Alanya couldn't tell if it was deliberate or unconscious.

In any case, it looked as if the tide of battle would favor the Argosseans. They continued to hammer the line of Aquilonians, the strength of their numbers and more numerous weapons cutting through the defenders in spite of an intense effort. Alanya watched, horror-struck, as sailors fell one after another. The mercenaries, more battle-hardened, took their toll on the pirates, but even so the numbers overwhelmed them.

It was becoming apparent that the pirates would break through the line, and those on the inside, still armed with nothing more than small stones, would be defenseless unless they could collect the weapons of the slain. The lifeboat neared shore, but looked as if it would be too late to be of much help.

Knowing that her life could depend on her own efforts, Alanya crept nearer one of the pirates Kral had defeated. Donial had taken the man's sword, but she thought she had seen a knife or dagger tucked inside his belt. He had fallen on his back, and blood caked his shirt and chest. She was pretty sure he was dead, but she wasn't positive. If she got near enough to reach his knife and he grabbed her instead, what then? The others were too busy fighting off the onslaught to help her.

She would just have to fend for herself, she supposed. As she neared the man, the stench of blood and death assailed her nostrils. He lay unmoving, his mouth gaping open, eyes staring unblinkingly at the blue sky. Doing her best to ignore his horrific aspect, she reached across his broad belly toward the hilt of the knife she could see there, its blade hidden beneath a wide crimson sash. Blocking out the sounds of combat and dying, she focused on the knife. Its hilt was silver and intricately carved, the tips of the guard curled slightly toward the blade.

As Alanya closed her fist around the hilt, she heard Donial cry out. Hurriedly, she snatched the knife from the sash and rose to her feet. Her brother had engaged one of the pirates. The man's cutlass slashed and cut, weaving a silvery pattern in the air. Donial did his best to keep up, swinging at the man, parrying his blows, but in spite of his lessons and practice, the buccaneer was clearly the more experienced swordsman by far.

She needed to do something, unable just to stand there while the first man her brother ever fought with a sword cut him down. But she could not reach his opponent, as the defenders had once again closed ranks, with Donial on the line beside Kral. She had a knife in her hand; she could throw it, but she knew there was an art to that. She scanned the ground quickly, looking for a cast-aside spear, crossbow, or other weapon she could use from a distance.

Down the beach, the men in the lifeboat were splashing ashore, and a group of Argosseans rushed to meet them, to stop them before they could offer aid to their comrades. One of the men remained in the boat, loosing crossbow bolts at the attackers while the others dragged the laden boat toward the sand.

That crossbow was too far away to help her, but there was sand right underfoot.

Tucking the knife in her belt for the moment, she squatted down and scooped up two fistfuls of the fine white sand. Moving as close behind Donial as she dared, she waited until the pirate had noticed her. He shot her a fierce, glowering grin, as if promising that she would come next, after Donial was killed. At that instant Alanya hurled both handfuls of sand right into his face.

Blinded, the pirate staggered back a couple of steps, spitting and blinking against the stuff in his eyes. Donial froze, until Alanya gave him a gentle shove. "Now's your chance!" she shouted. Seeming to wake up, Donial moved, taking advantage of the other's agony. He slashed with the cutlass and sliced the buccaneer down the chest, tearing his silk shirt and drawing a line of red across his skin. Realizing that wouldn't stop the man, he swung the sword back up, point first, shoving it into the pirate's exposed gut. Alanya thought the blade stuck there, but then Donial wrenched it free and the pirate slumped to his knees, dropping his own sword, hands clutching his midsection as the life flowed from him.

"You did it, Donial!" Alanya shouted, hoping she sounded encouraging. Donial's expression, when he turned to look at her, was anything but triumphant. She saw what appeared to be a deep sadness in his eyes. She knew he had long looked forward to experiencing battle for himself, but supposed that the reality of it didn't match his expectation. Then, almost as if in imitation of the man he had killed, he fell to his own knees, retching into the grass at the edge of the beach.

Alanya drew her dagger quickly and rushed to stand by his side, ready to protect him from any assault. But the battle, for the most part, seemed to be over.

A few of the sailors yet stood, each now wielding at least a single sword, and in some cases two. Likewise, a small handful of the mercenaries survived. Piles of dead Argosseans around them testified to their skills. The charming Captain Ferrin, Alanya noted with sorrow, had died early on, his corpse half-buried under others from both sides. Allatin, the first mate, yet lived. But as she watched, he took his cutlass and shoved its point into the sand, releasing its hilt so it stood there, quivering. Then he stepped away from it.

The signal it sent was clear. The dozen or so remaining from on board the *Restless Heart* surrendered to the Argosseans, who still numbered at least forty.

Alanya shuddered to think what the consequences of their action might be. She couldn't argue the sense of it—clearly, they were outmatched and had lost the fight. To continue would just mean that they would all die, instead of merely most of them.

Still, most of the men hesitated to agree to the surrender. Kral, bleeding from at least a dozen wounds, still held his weapons, and his aggressive stance suggested that he would be happy to continue fighting. Most of the mercenaries did the same. The sailors seemed more willing to go along with Allatin's surrender; most of them threw their weapons to the ground.

The presumed leader of the buccaneers approached Allatin. Around him, his men bristled with blades, but the leader himself slid his into a metal loop that dangled from a chain at his belt. "I accept your surrender," he said, "on behalf of the crew of the *Barachan Spur*. And I, Captain Kunios of the *Spur*, claim your ship as fair-won booty."

Some of the men grumbled, but Allatin only waited for a few seconds. "You'll need a crew," he said. "You will never get her repaired and under way without us."

"All who will swear fealty to me, and to the new *Barachan Spur,* may join my crew," Kunios declared. He wore a black shirt, or what was left of one. There had been a fresh cut across his left brow and cheek, now partnered with a newer one on his forehead and more on his exposed chest. He was among the tallest of the Argosseans, though still not much taller than Kral, and had a bulky muscularity. His hair was dark and unkempt, and his beard full. His eyes were red-veined and wild. Alanya suspected madness lurked behind them. "Any who refuse to so swear, speak up now so that you may be killed."

Alanya waited, thinking that perhaps some of the mercenaries would refuse such allegiance. Part of her almost hoped that Kral would. Not that she wanted to see him die, but she hated the idea of joining up with these bloodthirsty buccaneers, even for a moment.

She could read from Kral's posture and the determined set of his jaw that he hated it as much as she did. But he stuck his knife into his girdle—not quite as accepting of the situation as dashing it to the ground would have been, but surrender nonetheless. Donial's shoulders were slumped, his face blood-streaked, haggard, and dejected.

"Very well," Kunios said. "Welcome to the crew. My rules must be obeyed by all hands, on pain of death, keelhauling, marooning, or other such punishment, at my choice. We split all booty, in equal shares. We decide jointly where to sail, and when. At any time, I can be challenged for the captaincy—but I warn you, none have yet challenged me and lived to tell about it."

He looked at Allatin. "Who be you?"

"Allatin by name. First mate to Captain Ferrin, who lies there." He pointed toward the captain's lanky form.

"Well enough," Kunios replied. "Until we are all used to one another, I shall direct my orders for this lot to you, and expect you to deliver obedience in all things. First off, what cargo does the new *Spur* carry?"

"Wine, silks, furs, and skins," Allatin replied promptly. "Bound for markets in Stygia. Not much cargo this time—we were also a passenger vessel, carrying some of these before you to that same destination. There we hoped to pick up a full load, to sell in Aquilonia."

"So if I had my choice I would rather have taken you on the way back. But the choice was taken out of my hands when the *Barachan Spur* was broken up by a freak storm—the same storm, I wager, that grounded the new *Spur*."

"Aye," Allatin said. "It blew up from nowhere and forced us into that reef on which she rests."

"Most of her looks to be above water," Kunios noted.

"She's taking some on, through a break in her hull. But the reef holds her up, so the damage is not as bad as it might be."

Kunios turned his gaze from the ship to the people onshore, those left standing after the battle. When it landed on Alanya and held there, she felt it like a burn. His demented smile stabbed at her heart. "I am sorry to hear there isn't much cargo for us to sell," Kunios said. "But pleased to see that there are other . . . aspects, which may yet make this a favorable encounter for us."

She felt her flesh crawl at that remark, and at the searching stare that accompanied it. Kunios took a few steps closer to her, coming near enough that she could smell the blood and grime that covered him. "Very pretty," he said, almost as if speaking to himself, and yet loud enough for all to hear. "Likely the daughter of some nobleman who will pay a healthy ransom for her return."

Donial advanced angrily on the buccaneer. "She is my sister!" he said. "You keep your hands off her!"

Kunios laughed at Donial's rage. "Your sister, eh?" he said. "Then maybe it would be helpful to send your head to your father in a box, so he can see what might befall his lovely daughter if he fails to pay, well and fast."

"You will have to kill me if you hope to lay a finger on her," Donial threatened.

"Relax, boy," Kunios returned. "I have no intention

of touching her, nor does any other man on our crew. Our interest in a girl of her age is purely for the reward she might bring, so settle yourself down. I have no problem killing you, if you force me. But I might have need of another ship's boy, as I lost one in the storm."

Alanya had noted the way Kunios looked at her, and his consolations had a hollow ring. Donial scowled, but held his tongue. She could see that Kral had been poised, ready to spring on Kunios if he had made for her or for Donial. But Kunios moved away, and Kral allowed himself to relax again. Saving himself, no doubt, Alanya thought, for some other conflict yet to come.

She was positive that it would. And more likely sooner than later.

GORIAN AND SULLAS had hung back during the fighting, doing just enough not to rouse the suspicions of the mercenaries who worked for them, but keeping themselves away from real danger. As the ranks of the sailors and mercenaries had dwindled, however, Gorian had grown nervous. The pirate captain, Kunios, had been a fearsome warrior, and none had been able to stand against him. The Pict boy had done well, too, and Gorian had thought he might see a match-up between the two of them. But before that happened, he might have had to put his own life at risk, and that was out of the question. Allatin had surrendered just before the point that Gorian was going to insist on it.

Not that surrendering to Argossean pirates would help fulfill his mission. He had to assume that the crown Kanilla Rey wanted was still on its way to Stygia, or there already. But dead, there was nothing he could do to look for it. Alive, there was always a chance that he could somehow commandeer the ship, or depose its captain, or escape.

Particularly if he could count on Kanilla Rey's help.

He wasn't sure when he would be able to contact the sorcerer. He still had the rock fragment he needed, hanging safely around his neck. But he also needed privacy, and he had a feeling that if he tried to creep out of the camp tonight, the pirates would complain bitterly. Probably with the points of their swords.

He would just have to bide his time. The opportunity would arise, and he would have to be ready to seize it. At least both he and Sullas had been spared, and there were still half a dozen mercenaries pledged to serve him.

He would wait, and watch.

He really had no other choice.

15

THE COMBINED CREW of the new *Barachan Spur*
set to work fixing the ship that had formerly been the
Restless Heart. Palm trees were felled and cut into
planks. Nonessential sections of the ship were torn
apart so that lumber, pegs, nails, and other hardware
could be reused where needed.

Donial was put on a crew that pulled nails from
old boards by hand. His fingers went numb from the
effort, stinging and bleeding into the wood. Working
with Donial was the only other boy of his age, a
fourteen-year-old who said his name was Mikelo. He
was slight, with thick, light brown hair, brown eyes,
and a sad mouth, turned down at the corners in a per-
petual frown. Like most of the others, his clothing—
a tan linen shirt, striped pantaloons, and soft leather

boots—had not survived the shipwreck, march, and subsequent battle in one piece.

"How long have you sailed with these men?" Donial asked as they worked that afternoon.

"A bit more than a year, I think," Mikelo answered. "I was kidnapped from Kordava, just before my thirteenth birthday."

"Kordava—that is near the Pictish wilderness, is it not?" Donial wondered. He swatted at a flying insect—they swarmed around everyone and everything here, especially after the sun went down. In the Westermarck, relatively cool temperatures had seemed to keep the insect population at bay, and at home in Tarantia he was surrounded by a city's buildings and population. But here bugs were omnipresent. And annoying.

"Aye," Mikelo said. "Your friend is a Pict, no? I recognize the breed."

"My sister's friend, more than mine," Donial said, aware that even though Zingarans and Picts were natural enemies, so were Zingarans and Aquilonians. Those considerations seemed less important now, though, so far from home and all forced into the service of an Argossean buccaneer. "But yes, he is a Pict. We met him in the Westermarck."

Mikelo looked surprised. "You are a long way from there."

"And you a long way from Kordava."

"Not by choice," Mikelo reminded him.

Donial moved a little closer to him and lowered his voice. "Why have you not run away?"

"It is not so easily done," Mikelo said, adopting Donial's hushed tones. "Another Zingaran boy, Furelos, who was taken shortly after me, tried to jump ship when we landed once at Messantia. He thought he was unobserved, but one of the men spotted him and reported to Captain Kunios. By the time he reached shore, four men were waiting for him. He tried to outrun them, but they caught him anyway. Do you know what keelhauling is?"

"I heard your captain mention it," Donial said. "But I know not what the word means."

"They drag you by ropes down the length of the bottom of the hull, which on a ship is always studded with barnacles," Mikelo explained. "I had never seen it done, and still have not, as Furelos drowned before he had made it even a quarter of the way." The young man shuddered at the memory. "Some of the others said the captain had never done it either, just heard about it and wanted to see what it was like. His curiosity still burns, they told me, because Furelos died so quickly. So he itches for a chance to try it again."

"And this is a man those Argosseans willingly serve," Donial said, disgust welling up inside him. "People call Kral a savage, yet he has never done anything like that."

Mikelo shrugged. "It is a hard life, on the sea or

off it. Some just want to follow one who is powerful, regardless of what direction he leads."

"I suppose," Donial said. He didn't like it, but the fact was that he was doing the pirate captain's bidding, even now. He guessed Mikelo and some of the other men were no fonder of Kunios than he, but valued their lives enough to do as they were told. He swore it would only be temporary, though. He, Alanya, and Kral would escape this forced servitude at the first possible opportunity.

They moved on to the next plank, letting a couple of crewmen take the one they had finished with. As they shifted, Mikelo glanced at Alanya, whom Kunios had put to work mending tattered sails. She sat in the shade of one of the remaining palms, her legs outspread with the fabric she worked with covering them.

"That's your sister, eh?" Mikelo said, his gaze resting on her.

"Aye. Her name is Alanya."

"She's pretty," Mikelo said.

"I guess."

"No, she is. Really pretty." Mikelo stared at her a few moments longer. "It has been a long time since I've seen a girl at all," he said. "One anywhere near my age. Even then, not many were as lovely as she is."

"Stop staring at her," Donial urged. "I said she's my sister!"

Mikelo obediently looked back toward the board

they worked on. "Is she betrothed?" he asked. "Or married?"

"No!" Donial said sharply. After a few seconds, he decided his reaction had been overly harsh. "You want the truth, I think she is kind of sweet on Kral. But he does not know."

"The Pict?" Mikelo said with astonishment. "He's practically an animal!"

"He is not!" Donial insisted, swept up by a sudden fury. "He is as much a man as you. More so."

"Picts are headhunters," Mikelo countered. "They sleep in the mud. They eat human flesh."

"I thought you might know something about them, being from Kordava," Donial replied, fully aware that he had believed those same tales until a short while ago. "But I can see that you know only the same nonsense stories every Aquilonian child hears."

"Have you been to their villages?" Mikelo asked.

"No. But my father . . . my father used to go to them. He told us about them. He was friendly with some. And Kral has told us all about his life. He has never eaten people, or taken heads as souvenirs, or any of that."

"And you believe him?"

"More than I would believe whoever told you those lies. Had any of the people you heard them from ever been into the Pictish lands?"

Again, Mikelo shrugged. "I do not know. It's just what you hear, over and over, you know? I know no one who has met the king of Aquilonia, either, but I believe that he is a barbarian."

Donial felt vindication coming his way. "And do you imagine he would still be king if he engaged in the kinds of things you say Picts do? Are Cimmerians also animals, to you?"

"I know not," Mikelo said with a snicker. "All I know is, one sits on the throne of Aquilonia, not that of Zingara."

"For now," Donial said, unable to resist the dagger. "Until King Conan decides to expand his empire by taking over Zingara, too."

Mikelo's face turned red, and Donial braced himself, in case the boy attacked him. It had already been explained that fighting was forbidden among the ship's crew, however. Punishable by the loss of a hand, if one buccaneer raised a weapon against another, and by the loss of rations for mere fisticuffs. Donial was ready to risk it, but apparently Mikelo wasn't. He set to work again, suddenly seeming very interested in doing a good job on that particular plank.

Donial was happy to let it rest. He was pleased there was another boy his age on the crew, and didn't want to start out fighting with the fellow. If he had to be on the pirate's crew for a time, he might as well have a friend and possible ally who had been here for a while and knew how to get by.

But Mikelo's apparent interest in Alanya disturbed

him. As did, for that matter, what he perceived as Alanya's romantic interest in Kral. Though he had defended Kral, he still didn't think a savage was a proper match for a civilized young woman of Aquilonia. Anyway, Kral was so single-mindedly obsessed with his crown of teeth and bones, he barely seemed to notice that Alanya was even female, much less that she felt anything for him.

Donial still thought of his sister as a girl—older than him, but not by much, and certainly not of an age to be paired off with any man. Even the idea of it disturbed him.

He figured he would have to get used to it, someday.

But not today.

And not with some pirate's boy drooling over her.

WHAT KRAL DIDN'T know about ships was voluminous. He was frankly amazed that such a huge construction of wood and metal could float at all. He knew how to pilot a log canoe down a river, and had been out to sea briefly on rafts made of logs lashed together with vines. But until setting sail on the *Restless Heart,* he had never been on a serious ship, only glimpsing a couple from afar as they worked their way up or down the Western Ocean. Every moment the big craft stayed afloat was a bit of a revelation to him.

So he didn't volunteer any ideas or information about the reconstruction of the *Restless Heart,* which, as the days stretched on, seemed to become more and more complex. Without any way to hoist the vessel out of the water, men swam below to patch the hole torn by the reef's jagged edge. They nailed the used boards in place, then covered the seams and nails with pitch, taken from the ship's stores and heated over open flame.

But even after that repair work was done, Captain Kunios wasn't satisfied. He didn't want a three-masted carrack, shallow enough for river traffic, but something more akin to a sloop, the men said. None of these words meant anything to Kral, but he quickly got a sense of how much work was involved. He also learned how much the men feared Kunios, who, they hinted, had become ever more unhinged since losing his own vessel.

The carrack was big enough to haul cargo and men. Kunios wanted something lighter and swifter— able to dart after bigger ships, so that his men could board them and take only the most valuable booty back onto their own vessel. One of the Argosseans, a burly man named Bastri, with arms seemingly as long as an ape's and a great thatch of fur over his chest and belly, explained what the captain had in mind. "We strip out the forecastle," the man said. "And the pilot's cabin. And the railings. That's the easy part."

Kral nodded. He guessed it made sense—anyway, it seemed to, to Bastri. "Next, we take down the foremast and the mizzenmast. We'll remount that at the bow, as a new bowsprit. The canvas will have to be resewn, but once it is, it will all be stretched from either the mainmast or the bowsprit."

"What is the advantage of that?" Kral wondered.

"Speed and maneuverability," Bastri answered. "She will be twice the sea wolf she was before."

"I don't think Captain Ferrin intended her as a sea wolf," Kral said. "He used her for cargo and passengers."

"And he's dead, is he not?" Bastri added. "The old *Spur* was a fine fighting ship, but this new *Spur* will be the next best thing."

Kral looked at the ship, trying to picture what it would be like when all the work Bastri described was finished. And speculating on just how much time it would take.

Every day they stayed here, marooned on Shem's wild coast, two things were true.

The likelihood increased that Shemites would discover their presence. Then there would most likely be another battle. He, Alanya, and Donial had survived the first one. But the Shemites would not be limited to the few men who had survived a shipwreck and could keep reinforcing their side until victory was complete.

The other thing that worried Kral was that every day the Teeth of the Ice Bear got closer to Stygia—or, if it was already in that country, closer to being delivered into the hands of whoever had called for it to be taken there. Whoever that person was, he or she must have had some reason to want the Teeth.

And there was no *good* reason for the Teeth to be anywhere except safely in its cave beneath the Bear Clan's village. So that reason was a bad one.

Kral had meant to get the crown back before it could be used for any nefarious purpose. He didn't know how yet, or from whom he would take it. That would have to be figured out when the time came. But sitting there in Shem, working on a ship that would probably head back toward Argos and away from Stygia, only gave the thieves that much more time with the Teeth.

Kral was deeply indebted to Alanya and Donial. He liked them both, especially Alanya, more than he had ever liked anyone outside the Bear Clan. Maybe even more than anyone outside his own family.

But if it came down to a choice between his feelings for the two Aquilonians and his duty to the Pictish people as a whole, he would have to choose duty. The moment would come when he would have to try to escape this crew, and if that escape couldn't include his friends, he would have to leave them behind and strike out on his own for Stygia.

His only other option was challenging Kunios for the captaincy. The captain was a fearsome combatant, Kral knew. He thought he could take the man, but then again, many others had died trying. That in itself wasn't enough to make Kral hesitate. The problem was that if he lost, then there was no one left to go after the Teeth. And if he won, that still didn't mean he could dictate the destination of the ship. Kunios had said that the whole crew voted on that, and other buccaneers had confirmed that, in answer to Kral's discreet questions.

If he succeeded in taking over Kunios's job, then the others still might object if he decreed they were going immediately to Stygia. Then he'd be faced not just with one pirate to beat, but a whole shipful of them.

There just weren't any better options than escape. Followed, probably, by a long overland journey across Shem.

With or without Alanya and Donial.

Kral looked at the ship, pretending to care. But inside, his mood was cloudy and grim.

16

KUNIOS SURVEYED THE work being done to the captured ship. He liked the way it was taking shape, but not the speed at which the captives, and his own crew, were working. He wanted the *Barachan Spur* ready to sail. Too much time had already been wasted in that forsaken desert land. At any moment Kunios expected a Shemish army to crest the hill and attack.

He knew the men whispered about him, questioning his judgment. Even his sanity. It was ever thus, he acknowledged. Men doubted their leaders, but if thrust into the leadership role themselves, they would learn what a lonely, thankless task it was—surrounded by doubters, by those who believed they could do his job better than he.

Some just wanted to take the *Restless Heart* as she was, to patch the holes and put to sea. Never mind that she couldn't outrun an enemy galleon in that state, never mind that she was a merchant vessel and not a fighter. A plodder instead of a sprinter. Others had not wanted to stop and fight the *Heart*'s crew at all, preferring instead to continue overland back to Argos without delay.

And then there were the prisoners they had ended up with. Sailors, but also soldiers, a group of men who looked like they sold their arms, and their lives, to anyone with a cup of gold to offer. And not just them, but those others, the Aquilonian girl with her radiant blond hair, and her darker brother, and their Pictish friend. Kunios wondered desperately about them, about what had drawn them together and how they came to be on the *Heart.* But they refused to engage in conversation. They, too, he suspected, thought that he was not up to the job.

But they would learn better. Kunios had won his captaincy and kept it with a sharp mind and sharper cutlass. Enemies might lurk at every turn. His own crew might wish to cut his throat in his sleep. They would find that Kunios of Argos slept with one eye open, that he watched and waited, that he knew who was likely to betray him and could take the necessary actions to defend himself.

Even then, standing at the edge of the bustle, he could tell which crew members were content and which would like to bury their daggers in his back. As he watched, one of them, a laggard named Simloch, dropped a bucket of nails, overturning it into the sand. Simloch had hated Kunios for months, ever since he'd been disciplined for miscounting the booty from a captured ship.

"You!" Kunios shouted, pointing at the man. "You dropped those nails just to slow down repairs to the ship, didn't you?"

Simloch looked at him, sudden terror masking his face. "No, Captain," he said. "It's just . . . you made me nervous, starin' at me like that, and—"

"Nervous?" Kunios interrupted. He barked a fierce laugh. "What good is a nervous seaman?"

"It's only a few nails, Captain," Simloch protested, scrabbling at the fallen nails with both hands. "I'll have 'em picked up quick."

"With your teeth," Kunios ordered.

"What?"

"Pick them up with your teeth, man. You've got to learn to do things right the first time."

"But Captain . . ."

That was what Kunios had been waiting for. The willful disobedience of a direct command. "You refuse?"

"Captain, I . . ."

Kunios drew his cutlass and stormed across the gap separating them. Simloch dropped the nails in his hands and reached for his dagger. Kunios gave him a half second, until the dagger cleared its scabbard, then he attacked.

Simloch was a stout man, bare-chested, with white hair and a clean-shaven chin. He threw up the dagger to block Kunios's blow, and his protruding gut shook. Kunios envisioned driving the point of his cutlass straight into that round belly. But the others were watching now, and he thought they should see an appropriate display of swordsmanship. Even against such a worthless foe, proper technique could be applied.

So he wove a shining web with his blade, dazzling poor Simloch, whose dagger was barely up to the task of parrying. It would not have been, had Kunios not chosen to extend the fight. His cutlass swooped up like a gull with a freshly caught fish, swung down like slashing rain, arced from one side or the other. Dizzied by the onslaught, Simloch tried to appeal to his captain. But to no avail.

When Kunios was sure he had impressed all observers with his technique, he let the cutlass blade drop below Simloch's upraised dagger and sliced across the man's exposed belly. A line of red followed the sword tip's path. Simloch cried out, and Kunios dealt him a killing blow to the neck.

When the seaman fell, the whole camp was silent, looking on.

Kunios returned his sword to its place on his belt.

"You see?" he shouted. "You see what rebellion will get you? Do you?"

A few halfhearted calls of "Aye, Captain," came in response.

"All of you!" Kunios demanded. "Do you see?"

This time, the men thundered out their answer. "Aye, Captain!"

Better, Kunios thought. For another day or two, they were his. None would dare betray him now. Not, at least, until the memory of this demonstration slipped from their feeble minds.

"Someone pick up those nails!" Kunios called. "And get rid of that body. Sight of it makes me sick."

ALANYA SAT ON the beach, massaging her hands. Her fingers were cramped from sewing—first repairing clothing belonging to a few of the buccaneers, then reshaping sails to meet the new requirements of the refitted *Restless Heart*. The canvas was much harder to work with. She had to force the needle through with all her might, often pricking herself in the process. Her shoulders ached from the constant bending over her work, and even her legs complained from being seated on the ground so much.

She didn't complain out loud, though. She knew that Donial's hands had been worn almost to the bone by his first task. Now he and Mikelo had been assigned to other duties, on the ship, scrambling and crawling into spaces too small for the larger seamen, or up the rigging. Still, her brother was in just as much pain as she was, his muscles being forced into activities every bit as foreign to his experience as day after day of needlework was to hers.

She longed to be away from here, back in her home in Tarantia. During the night, she had even dreamed of it. Father had been there, and Cheveray, Kral, and Donial. They had been sitting in the court-yard, with a soft breeze blowing white flower petals all around them. She had been filled with a sensation of loving warmth that she never wanted to end. Waking up here on this desolate stretch of beach, a captive once more, she had been so disappointed she had nearly wept.

As she sat there, rubbing her hands and wishing that fate hadn't thrown them into their situation in the first place, Kral came and squatted beside her. Of the three of them, he was the one faring best—his skin even more tanned than it had been back in his home-land, where the skies were often cloudy and gray, his wounds healing over, his muscles firm and round. He had been assigned heavy labor, lifting and carrying things, mostly, which suited him, and he went on oc-casional hunting forays to supplement the food stores from the *Restless Heart.*

"Your hands hurt." It was an observation, not a question.

"Yes," she said. "So do Donial's."

"His will toughen up," Kral said. "He will get calluses on them. He'll be fine."

"We all will be," Alanya said hopefully.

Kral nodded and touched her arm sympathetically. "I should have fought harder."

"There was nothing more you could have done," Alanya said. "No one could have defeated enough pirates to make the difference."

"Your brother killed a man," Kral said. "Has he talked about it to you?"

Alanya had tried to raise the subject a couple of times, in the brief periods they'd had together. So far, without success. "No," she replied. "He has not wanted to. I think he's embarrassed that it made him sick."

"He shouldn't be," Kral said. "I have done it many more times than him, and I still don't like it. Anyway, it was not just the killing that made him sick. It was battle nerves. I have seen that happen many times. Everyone's stomach is churning during a fight like that. Some can contain it better than others, that's all. Especially if they have done it before."

A question Alanya had never asked Kral—because she had been afraid of the answer—sprang to her lips before she could stop it. "How many . . . how many people have you killed, Kral?"

He looked off to sea and contemplated the question. "I lost count during the battle the other day," he said after a time. "But probably seven, or eight, then. Before that, the soldier in Tarantia. A few at Koronaka, at the wall there. Maybe fifteen in all."

"But you do not know for sure."

"No," he said simply.

She didn't understand how that could be. She thought that the taking of another human's life should leave a mark on a person, like a tattoo or a brand. It should not be something done lightly, without serious understanding of its consequence.

The marks on Kral, if they were there at all, were internal. She couldn't look at them and tote them up.

Apparently, neither could he.

"You will not like hearing this," he said, after they had both sat in silence a few minutes. The late-afternoon sun gleamed off his flesh, making him look like a golden statue by the beach. "But I would kill fifteen more, to protect you. Or to get the Teeth back. And I would do it happily."

Alanya understood why he didn't think she would like hearing that. And for the most part, he was right. She didn't want to think about him killing anyone, on her behalf.

But she thought that she would do the same for him, or for Donial. Perhaps not happily. But if it was their lives, or another's, she would choose theirs, every time. No matter what the cost to herself.

What was that? Love? Family?

She didn't know. She wasn't sure her friends in

Tarantia—the "civilized" girls she knew—would even recognize her any longer, or understand the impulses that drove her.

The whole experience was changing her, undeniably. Whether that change was for better or worse wasn't within her power to judge. *Leave that for someone else,* she thought. *Someone who has the luxury of judgment.*

For her, survival was the issue. Judgment was for people sitting safely inside comfortable homes.

"DO YOU WANT to escape?"

Donial looked at Mikelo, astonished that the young man would even suggest it. "I thought you said it was impossible."

"Not necessarily impossible," Mikelo replied. "Just very difficult. And very dangerous."

"It does not seem that going off on the ship with these pirates will exactly be safe," Donial noted. He looked at the big mounds of sand on the beach where all the bodies from the other day's battle had been buried. He had killed one of those men. He wished it had been more. Kunios, especially. "Especially if Captain Kunios wants to ransom my sister to my father, since he is dead."

"Then he will likely just auction her off somewhere," Mikelo told him. "Which would be awful."

Donial already knew the Zingaran had a crush on

Alanya—he didn't want to listen to the details again. "That is not going to happen," he stated flatly.

"The only way to be sure of that is to get away from here before we cast off," Mikelo said. Suddenly Donial understood why Mikelo had changed his mind about escape. He wanted to "rescue" Alanya and make her feel indebted to him. He understood, but he cared less about the motivation than about the possibility of success. "And the ship is going to be ready soon," Mikelo added.

Donial scanned the horizon. Tall grass spread out into the far distance. Etched across the edge of the vast grassy plain was a dark line that might have been forest. But anyone crossing that grass would leave a distinct track, like the Argosseans had made when they came here.

Donial and Mikelo had been sent from the new *Barachan Spur* to shore to deliver stored food to those left onshore. Alone on the lifeboat, midway between, it was safe enough to talk about such things. But they needed to finish up soon because several of the buccaneers were waiting for them on the beach.

"Do you have an actual plan?" Donial asked as he rowed.

"More of an idea than a plan, I guess. Here it is. The ship will be ready to sail by morning. It looks ready now, but Kunios will want to wait until morning light to cast off. He will be anxious to get under way, if I know him. So my idea is, tonight, when most of the Argosseans are on board and only a few guards remain behind on land, we slip away. Instead of going straight across the grass, we take to the water and walk along the shore for a few miles. The waves will cover any noise we might make and obscure our tracks. Only after we are well out of sight of the ship do we cut across the grass. In the morning, by the time anyone realizes we have gone, Kunios will be so ready to leave, he won't want to spend much time looking for us. When there are no visible tracks, he will just cast off. Then we can cut across Shem to Argos, then Zingara or Aquilonia. Or we can take the longer route, through Koth and Ophir if you want to avoid Argos."

"Actually, we need to get to Stygia," Donial said.

Mikelo shivered in spite of the hot sun blazing down on them. "I would be happy never to set foot there again."

"I never have," Donial told him. "But I have no choice in the matter. There is . . . something that Kral has to do there."

"So you plan to stay with the Pict?"

"Aye," Donial said. "He goes where we go."

"Your sister might like Kordava."

"She will probably never find out," Donial replied. Fortunately, they were approaching the beach, and he jumped out of the boat to haul it in. As the water splashed around his thighs, he thought of Mikelo's scheme.

It just might work—if he was right about the majority of the buccaneers spending the night on the boat. If they didn't, then it was probably doomed to failure.

He didn't want to find out what keelhauling was really like—certainly not from the vantage point of the keelhauled.

But he also didn't want to set sail on the *Barachan Spur,* bound for parts unknown.

KRAL AND ALANYA both agreed to the escape plan, once Donial was able to explain it to them. Kral seemed a bit more reluctant than Alanya, or maybe just more realistic about their prospects, but he indicated his willingness to go along with it. Alanya, already sick of Kunios's frequent and unabashed stares, was more enthusiastic. Both suspected that Kunios was half-mad, at least. His one-sided battle with his own sailor made it even more apparent, although Kral had expressed grudging admiration of the pirate captain's swordsmanship.

When night fell, however, a minor problem revealed itself. Kunios intended to sleep aboard the ship in his new cabin, and he took a crew out to finish some last-minute preparations for sailing at first light. But the bulk of the pirate crew, as well as the sailors and mercenaries from the *Restless Heart,* would be staying onshore until morning. Which meant more guards posted and less opportunity to slip away unseen.

Even so, Mikelo indicated his eagerness to try. Donial brought the news to Alanya and Kral, and they both agreed as well. Alanya could barely eat dinner, so consumed was she with nervousness. Still, she knew it was important to maintain the pretense that everything was fine, so she tried to force down as much of the dried, salted pork and hard biscuits as she could. When one of the buccaneers asked her if she was ill, she replied that she was just anxious about setting off to sea in the morning. The man seemed to accept that as an answer and moved on.

It felt like days passed before the camp settled down for the night. Alanya, Donial, and Kral had always slept near the edge of the group anyway, since they were not really seafaring types and felt a bit like outsiders among these others. That night, Mikelo picked a sleeping spot nearer them than he had on other occasions. They all bedded down at the usual time, and Alanya closed her eyes, listening to the jokes, boasts, and lies of the pirates (and the crew from the old *Restless Heart,* who seemed already to be blending in with the Argosseans), as she pretended to sleep.

Eventually, the camp was quiet. She actually dozed for a time, despite her nerves. When Kral gently nudged her shoulder, though, she woke immediately, alert and aware of the situation.

Mikelo crouched nearby, and Donial was pushing himself up onto hands and knees. They had agreed to lie down in the clothes they planned to wear on their escape, with the food and weapons they planned to bring close at hand. All had chosen dark clothing, and Alanya had also picked a black cloak to help hide her in the night. Her pouch contained her mirror, of course, which so far she had managed to keep hidden.

Without speaking, they all started away from the group of sleeping men. Alanya heard snores, men twisting and writhing in their sleep, even one man who seemed to be laughing to himself. But as she scanned the camp, by light of the crescent moon and a smoldering campfire, she didn't see anyone who looked awake—not even the guard, sitting up by the palms at the top of the beach, whose chin rested on his chest. Maybe the absence of their captain from the camp tonight meant that security would be more lax than usual.

She could hope, anyway.

The beach was flat, curving in a gentle arc. The four companions moved stealthily toward the southeast, toward Stygia and away from Argos, then cut down to the water. As soon as they reached it they waded in. The water chilled Alanya's legs, but she appreciated Mikelo's idea—the steady surf covered the sound of their getaway, and the water wiped away their tracks the moment they were made.

As they put more and more distance between

themselves and the camp, Alanya began to relax. This was going to work. She allowed herself a private smile.

She started to turn to Kral to say something—the first words that would have passed between any of them since they left their sleeping areas.

But as soon as she opened her mouth, before any sound could come out, she heard the shouts from the direction of camp. When she spun around to look back that way, she saw a swarm of buccaneers heading down the beach toward them. Moonlight glinted coldly on the blades of their swords.

Kral grabbed her hand. "Run!" he cried, tugging on her.

Alanya ran.

17

KRAL KNEW THAT, given his head start, he could outrun the pirates who chased them.

They were used to life on board ship, where the longest run was only a few yards. Possibly they could outswim him, but he wasn't even sure about that.

But he could run for days—literally—at top speed, for hours at a time. If he paced himself he could run from daybreak to sunset without stopping once. There was no way the pirates could stop him if he went all out. He wouldn't have to stop until he was most of the way to Stygia, and their legs would give out long before that.

There was one problem with that, however.

At the moment, Donial was ahead of him. Donial was a sprinter, one of the fastest Kral had ever seen.

He could leave those pirates eating his dust, although Kral doubted he could sustain that pace for very long. He was a product of civilization, after all, not accustomed to running for his very life. But he could put some real distance between himself and the pirates, and maybe lose them.

That left Alanya and Mikelo to worry about.

Kral didn't much care what happened to Mikelo, except that their whole plan, however flawed, had been his idea. He guessed he owed the youngster something for that.

But in spite of his earlier resolve, he didn't think he could leave Alanya behind. He held her hand, warm and pliant in his grip, and tried to tug her along with him. They eased out of the surf and onto the sand, since speed mattered more than stealth at that point. Even sand wasn't ideal, and he was trying to work them all toward the grass, where they could run faster still.

He had slept for a couple of hours. But during that time, he had been consumed by a dream. In that dream, he had seen a man—himself, and yet not himself, in the way that only dreams can do—living on the edge of an island far out in the Western Ocean. He looked farther to the west, off to sea, and he saw a thick, dark mass of clouds coming his way. He shouted to his fellows, all Picts, stunted and dark, but he could find no voice. Looking out to sea again, he discovered that the clouds had taken the shape of a bear.

Some part of his mind tried to give meaning to the images even as he was dreaming them. Legend had it that the Picts had once lived on islands in the Western Ocean, islands that had become mountain ranges after the Great Cataclysm reshaped the world. The huge gray/white bear that lumbered menacingly toward the island could only be the Ice Bear.

Then others on the island saw the bear's approach as well. They screamed and tried to run, but still no voices could be heard. Kral could hear only the roar of the wind, growing louder as if it was the very breath of the massive bear. The wind was cold; branches iced up and snapped under its assault, naked flesh froze. Kral realized that he wore a bearskin, and he drew it more tightly around himself. Even so, he shivered with the chill that surrounded him.

As the bear came nearer, the very sea itself froze solid. The bear was no mere shape in the clouds now. It had form, and weight, and the frozen ocean waves cracked and shrieked under its tread. In its fur Kral could see icicles longer than the tallest trees on the island, and in its eyes, he saw cold disregard for any unfortunates in its path. The Ice Bear was a force of nature, as unfeeling as wind or rain or flame. And still, it came on.

Picts tried to run, tried to leap into the sea on the other side of the island and swim for the mainland. But the sea had frozen on that side, too. They only slipped and slid, and when they were able to get far enough away, the ice cracked under them, sending them hurtling beneath its surface, where they were trapped. The dream-Kral watched this with horror, but he made no move to join them. He simply stayed where he was, as if cemented to the spot by the ice that was everywhere now.

The Ice Bear was upon him. Its claws raked the island's shore as it came, its cold breath washed over him. Kral thought his own eyeballs would freeze and crack in his head. One great paw hovered above him, about to drop down, and surely he would be killed when it did—

Then he awoke, with Mikelo shaking his shoulder. Kral nodded once, instantly alert, and went to wake Alanya.

While running, he remembered the dream. He knew what it meant—he needed to save the Teeth of the Ice Bear, to return it to its proper spot. If he failed to do so, the Ice Bear would come back, and disaster would follow in its wake. Kral rolled over his earlier decision in his mind—that he would put the Teeth first, no matter what. That his own escape was of paramount importance, and other considerations had to be relegated to second place.

And then he looked at Alanya, her golden hair bouncing in the moonlight as she ran, her face serious, giving every ounce of strength she could to the effort. If only she hadn't tried so hard. If only he didn't know that if he asked her, she would tell him to go, to leave her behind, to find the Teeth and get it back where it belonged. She would be fine, she would insist. Run, Kral, run while you can, she would say. He was certain of it.

Which was why he couldn't ask her. And why he couldn't just leave her behind, let his legs stretch their full distance, and leave the pirates wondering if he was man or gazelle.

He glanced at her again, as these thoughts rushed through his busy mind, and their eyes locked briefly, then Alanya was pulling her hand free from his grip. "You can get away," she said, between huffs of tired breath. Almost as if she had known his thoughts. "Go on, Kral! Please!"

"No," he started to protest. But the look in her eyes was imploring. With just that, just the message delivered by those two blazing blue eyes on a dark night, she told him that she understood the urgency of his quest, and she beseeched him to carry it through to its conclusion.

Kral felt that by leaving her behind, he would be losing a piece of his heart, as well. It was an almost physical pain in his chest. He didn't let it slow him down, though, didn't hesitate to extend his legs more, to pump his arms faster, to feel the ground rushing beneath him as he raced, liberated and hurting, into the night.

• • •

ALANYA HAD FELT herself slowing Kral down, felt him trying to tug her along faster. But she was worn out. She had not slept much at all, her body was still tense and stiff from all the sitting and sewing of the last few days, and she had barely eaten today, so her body had no fuel to draw on.

Donial had already far outpaced them, and even Mikelo was moving ahead a little. But Kral was the one who truly needed to get away. He was the only one who could return the Pictish crown to its proper place, and he needed to do it before whatever disaster was in the offing took place. What happened to Alanya mattered to Donial, to Cheveray, maybe to Kral, and a few friends back in Tarantia, but it didn't have any greater overall significance. Kral might be saving the world, or at least part of it. Alanya was only saving Alanya.

So she had to let him go. Without her to worry about, she knew he could lose the pursuing buccaneers. Maybe Donial could, too. If she let them catch her, maybe even Mikelo would escape.

Not that she would give up, or voluntarily turn back. But her lungs were beginning to ache, and she thought her legs would cramp up at any moment. She wasn't going to last much longer.

She kept her head down, kept running as long as she could. A month ago, she wouldn't have made it half that far. But her adventures had already made her stronger, not just physically but mentally, emotionally.

She had fought for things worth having, and she knew how to make that decision now. She was able to make a decision that, a month ago, would have paralyzed her—to guarantee Kral's safety she would risk her own.

Freedom was worth having, and she would fight with every fiber of her being for it. But she would not slow down others fighting for the same thing. She couldn't do that and live with herself after.

She could see by Kral's face that he didn't want to go without her. But he understood the sense of it just the same. He gave a barely perceptible nod—one he might not even have been aware of himself—and sped up, pulling away from Alanya almost instantly.

Alanya gave Kral a few minutes to build up a good lead. Then she turned inland, running through tall, thick grasses that tore and pulled at her wet legs. The pirates were gaining ground fast. She didn't think it would be long before they caught up. So she wanted to make them chase after her, or at least split up, giving the others a better shot at escape.

She ignored the clawing grasses and hurried toward the far side of the field, where she thought a dark line indicated some inland forest. If she could make it there . . .

But, no, she didn't think she would. Already her breathing was ragged, her heart slamming so hard in her rib cage she thought it would burst. Her pace faltered, a combination of the thick grass underfoot and

the deep weariness in her limbs. She could hear pirates close behind, the rustle of the grass as they cut
through it, their harsh breaths and muttered curses.

Pressing on, Alanya tried to imagine herself free
of them, back home in Tarantia, with Donial and Kral
around her. Maybe sitting beside a fireplace on a
winter's night, hot mugs of cider close at hand . . .

And then a hard fist slammed into her shoulder.
She went tumbling in the grass, winding up sprawled
facedown. The knee of one of the pirates pressed into
the small of her back, his breath hot and foul on her
neck . . .

GORIAN KNEW IT was his best chance. With most
of the camp chasing after those stupid kids, and Kunios and some of his crew on the ship, he could slip
away and contact Kanilla Rey. He made sure no one
was watching—not even Sullas, who stood, like most
of the rest, looking into the distance to observe the
pursuit.

Fishing the stone from underneath his shirt, he
backed away from camp, into the darkness on the other
side of the palms. Once clear of the beach, he walked
gingerly through the grass, torn between the desire to
move fast and the urgency of not making much noise.
Most of the camp was awake now. The few who hadn't
gone after the youngsters were talking, discussing the

chase, wagering on the outcome. Even so, he didn't want to take any chances on one of them hearing him.

On the ship, he saw lanterns moving about. They had heard the fuss, even over there, he guessed, and Kunios was sending someone back to investigate. That made speed all the more necessary to Gorian, who would want to be back at camp before anyone returned from the ship.

A few minutes later, he found, by the moon's dim glow, a slight depression in the meadow. Lowering himself to the ground, he was out of sight of the camp and the ship. This, he thought, would have to suffice. He cut his flesh, pressed his hand against the rock. As loudly as he dared, he spoke the required phrases while staring into the chunk of stone.

"It has been a long time, Gorian," Kanilla Rey's voice answered. "I have been getting worried." Once again, Gorian thought he sensed the presence of the sorcerer, here in the grassy dip, but he could see nothing out of the ordinary.

"Much has happened," Gorian said. "A storm blew us toward shore, where we went aground on a reef. We had to abandon the ship. Then we were attacked by Argossean buccaneers, who have taken over. We are all prisoners now, and have been forced—those of us still alive, at any rate—to join their crew. We are still beached, but setting sail on the morn."

"But no longer bound for Stygia?"

"I think not," Gorian answered. "More likely for Argos."

"This is very bad news, Gorian," Kanilla Rey's voice said.

"I know," Gorian replied. "This is the first chance I have had to contact you."

"Something must be done," Kanilla Rey said. "Listen closely . . ."

DONIAL FELT LIKE he had been running all his life.

He should have been pacing himself better, he knew. He had sprinted full out, and now his legs were weakening, his strides faltering. He had heard Alanya fall, a while before. Then, a short time after that, Mikelo. He knew that Kral, who had passed him earlier, was still out in front. Donial had almost reached the distant tree line, but when he glanced behind him he saw that there were still four pirates on his tail, and they weren't giving up.

Kral, he guessed, was already deep in the woods and probably safe. The only pirates still on the hunt were behind Donial, and he doubted if they'd have the strength to keep going after Kral. They were slowing, too, visibly weakening, just as he was.

Determined to go on, he kept his legs moving in spite of the pain. The trees drew ever closer. There, perhaps he could find a hiding place. Out in the grass, even in the faint moonlight, he was too exposed. The flaw in Mikelo's plan was that it relied too heavily on no one noticing their absence until they were long gone. Better, probably, to have waited for another chance, where there were places to hide from pursuers.

He remembered the things that Mikelo had told him about the other young man who had tried to escape. The attempted keelhauling, the drowning. And he thought about his sister, in the clutches of that pirate captain. Could he abandon her to whatever evil torture the man might dream up next?

The forest, and possible salvation, was tantalizingly close ahead. He risked a backward glance. The pirates were still far enough back. He could make the trees. They were no guarantee of safety, but they were the closest he had to one.

He thought once more of his sister, and he let his legs tangle together, dumping him onto the grass just before the tree line. Spent, he tried to force himself back to his feet. Before he could, the four buccaneers surrounded him and stopped, glaring down at him.

"Let's show the boy how much we appreciate our late-night run," one offered.

"Captain Kunios will want to punish the kid himself," another said.

"Yeah, but he ain't here."

The others laughed at that. Donial didn't like that laughter at all. There was a distinctly sinister edge to it. He had let himself be caught because he wanted to

be taken back, wanted to be able to help Alanya if
things got bad for her.

If they killed him here, then his sacrifice was for
naught.

He wanted to speak up in his own defense, but
what could he say? He had, in fact, made them run,
likely far longer than seamen were used to, or happy
about. He had been trying to escape. Everything they
complained of, he had done intentionally.

Instead of defending himself, Donial said the first
thing that came to mind. "You might have caught me
sooner if you weren't a scurvied, bowlegged bunch
of sea dogs."

His taunt had the expected effect. Swords slid from
scabbards, and one of the men spat into the grass.
"Killing you is going to be much more fun than chasing you, pup," he said.

Donial yanked his own sword free. He had only
used it once, in real battle. That had been one against
one, and Alanya had helped.

Now it was four to one.

Donial swallowed hard and braced for the worst.

18

FROM HIS VANTAGE point among the trees, Kral listened intently. Believing that Donial was close behind, he had taken cover past the tree line. It was not a dense forest, as he had hoped, just a thin veil of trees along the banks of a shallow creek. There, he had hoped to wait for Donial, so that the two of them could stay together. He doubted that anything in Donial's life had prepared him for survival on his own, out in the wilderness. With Kral's help, however, Donial would be fine—and it was entirely possible that Kral could in turn use an ally as he sought out the Teeth.

But from what he heard now, not only had Donial stumbled and been caught, he was about to be killed for his trouble. As much as Kral wanted to get away, he couldn't just stand and listen to that. Arguing with himself every step of the way, he worked his way quickly back through the trees, to the edge of the grassy plain.

Donial, his back to Kral, held his sword out, his feet widely spaced. He actually looked like he knew what he was doing, Kral thought.

Still, four against one, and that one just a boy, green and untested. If nothing else, Kral could even the odds a bit.

Drawing the sword he had taken from the pirate camp, he loosed a full-throated war cry and hurled himself from the trees, slashing at the nearest of the buccaneers. The man saw him at the last moment and threw up his own sword to block the blow. Kral's blade was deflected, but the tip snaked down and sliced into the pirate's arm. The man grunted in pain and dropped back a step.

Shoulder to shoulder with Donial, now, Kral faced the four men.

"It does not have to be this way," he said.

"Meaning what?" one of the buccaneers asked.

"We will surrender and go back to camp peacefully," Kral explained. "Or you can try to fight us, and all die right here."

"I say we fight," another one replied. But the one Kral had cut was holding his hand over the wound and grimacing with pain. A third pirate turned to peer back toward the camp and the ship.

"Maybe we should accept their surrender," he said. "Captain Kunios will want to deal with them himself, anyway."

"Aye," the fourth one agreed. "No need to wear ourselves out any further with this lot."

Kral felt Donial's glare burning into him. He knew the boy would view his surrender as a betrayal. To explain, he turned to Donial and silently mouthed one word. "Alanya."

Donial nodded, seemingly catching on.

Kral had figured out that Donial had allowed himself to be caught—he could have made the trees, after all—because he was worried about what might happen to his sister if he didn't. So he could hardly complain if Kral did the same thing, and for the same reason.

"All right," the first pirate said. "Have it your way. Throw down your weapons."

"I said we would surrender," Kral answered. "But we keep our weapons, at least until we get to camp. If you think I trust you for a second, you are wrong."

The buccaneers nodded their assent, and the six of them began the long walk back toward camp.

ALANYA WAS ASTONISHED to look up and see Kral and Donial walking back to the pirate camp, still armed, and in the company of four rogues who looked as if they could barely stay upright.

The sky was beginning to lighten in the east. The night had been long, eventful, and wearying. She still had not slept, but after having been escorted back to camp, was lashed with thick, greasy rope to one of the palm tree trunks. After an hour or so, Captain Kunios and a few of the others who had planned to spend the night on the *Barachan Spur* came ashore. Kunios asked pointed questions of the pirates, particularly the one who had been on guard, and threw some barbed looks her way, but did not address her directly.

Mikelo was brought back to camp about the same time. Kunios did speak to him. He backhanded Mikelo across the face, knocking the young man to the ground. Mikelo got up, blood starting to show at the corners of his mouth, and he was pushed down again, made to sit on the ground, surrounded by the people he had just tried to run away from. He wasn't bound, but Alanya didn't think he would be running again anytime soon.

But . . . Kral and Donial looked as if they were returning voluntarily. She could not imagine any other reason they would be allowed to keep their own weapons. Why would they have done that?

Apparently she would not get the chance to ask them, at least not right away. They were brought into the camp but kept some distance from her. One of the pirates who had accompanied them held a hushed conversation with Captain Kunios, who glared at them, then indicated they should be held away from her. Neither was bound, but they did surrender their weapons, and armed men surrounded them.

With the dawning of the new day, the camp began to bustle with activity. Lifeboats made trips over to the *Barachan Spur*—Alanya on the first trip, Mikelo, Kral, and Donial on the second. Some of the pirates who had spent the night on the ship came back to help strike the camp, while several of the mercenaries and sailors from the original *Restless Heart* were brought with Alanya and the others to the ship, to work on making her ready to sail.

She couldn't help worrying about when Kunios's punishment would be dealt out. From Mikelo's stories she knew that the pirate had a fierce temper and did not brook disobedience. She had seen that for herself, when he disciplined a man who had simply made a mistake. The man seemed blood-crazed and unstable to her. So far, the escape attempt she and her friends had made was the first sign of genuine rebellion she had observed, so she didn't know precisely how the captain would respond. She didn't expect to like it.

Even so, she wouldn't have had it any other way. Once they were on board the ship, she guessed, opportunities for escape would be much more limited. She was glad they had at least tried to get away rather than meekly accepting the situation as it was. And while she thought she understood why Kral and

Donial had allowed themselves to be captured, she couldn't help wishing that they hadn't. Regardless of what Captain Kunios had in mind for her, she could take care of herself. And as long as he believed she had parents who might pay a ransom for her, he was unlikely to hurt her.

On board, activity was frantic, and while she, Mikelo, Donial, and Kral were excluded from the preparations and still not allowed weapons, they were no longer kept away from each other. She was sitting in the stern, trying to keep out of the way, when the others came to join her.

"Why are you here?" she demanded, when they approached. "You two could have gotten away!"

"You are my sister," Donial said, as if that explained it all. "I could not just abandon you."

"There will be other chances," Kral said. "And we will all go together when we do."

"What about the—" Alanya had almost said "Teeth," but caught herself, realizing that Mikelo didn't know the nature of Kral's quest. "What about your destination?"

"I did not say we would wait very long for our next chance," he said, with a smile. "Just that we would wait for the right one."

"But . . ." She didn't complete the thought. She knew Donial could be stubborn, and supposed that applied to Kral as well. Maybe to all males.

"You should not be left alone with these pirates,"

Mikelo said. Alanya didn't think he had intentionally allowed himself to be caught, but maybe he had. Or maybe he just preferred to let her think so. She knew, by the way he looked at her and tried to spend time around her, that he was fond of her.

She didn't think she could ever return that feeling. He was nice enough, but the physical attraction he obviously felt for her was not shared.

"I would have been fine," she protested.

"You do not know Kunios," Mikelo said. "You might not have been injured, until he learned that you have no family to pay a ransom. But once he did, anything could happen. You could be flogged to within an inch of your life, sold to slavers, drowned, or marooned."

All those possibilities had occurred to Alanya. She had also decided that, alone or with her friends, she would escape the buccaneers before any of those things happened. Even if she had to get away by jumping overboard in the middle of the ocean, taking her chances with sharks and drowning. Better to die free than to live in tortured servitude.

They were sitting together, discussing these things in hushed tones, when they heard the first pirate die.

AT KANILLA REY'S suggestion, Gorian had subtly hinted to some of the buccaneers that the former crew, including his mercenaries, of the *Restless Heart* should do most of the preparation for sailing. They were used to the ship, he mentioned, ignoring the fact that it had been considerably changed. Besides, with them working hard, the *Barachan Spur*'s pirates could relax a little before setting off. Striking the camp would be a simple matter, not very taxing. By the time they reached the ship, the hard work would have been done.

Not all of the pirates agreed with this reasoning, and there were some he didn't get the chance to talk to. But enough of them went along with the idea, and some even told their friends. Gorian heard a few snickering that they were making the new men do all the difficult work.

Which was just fine with Gorian. He allowed himself to be taken over on one of the early boats. Most of his mercenaries were on that one or the next. When that boat had arrived and the sailors, mercenaries, and a handful of the *Barachan Spur*'s pirates were busy rigging and hoisting the sails, he told the nearest mercenary that it was time to act. They had discussed the plan previously, and he had assured them that they'd have Kanilla Rey's assistance when the time came.

Moresh, a Poitainian with a neck like a bull's and arms corded with steely muscle, made the first move. He moved close to a pirate, who was busy making fast a rigging line, and drew his poniard, driving it deep into the buccaneer's gut while the man had his hands full of taut rope. The man let out a pained groan and released the rope, which flew from his hands.

Moresh rammed his elbow into the dying man's face, knocking him over the side and into the sea. On cue, the rest of the mercenaries, and those few of Captain Ferrin's sailors whom Gorian had trusted, went into action. Each one struck down the pirate nearest to him. An alarm was sounded, and the remaining pirates drew cutlasses and gave more of a battle than the first lot had. Steel clashed against steel, men shouted oaths and screamed with pain when they were cut. A couple of the sailors went down under pirates' attacks, and Gorian watched his tiny crew become smaller yet.

Which was when Kanilla Rey's promised aid came into play. Gorian tore the hanging stone from beneath his shirt and held it up in his hand, squeezing it so tightly that it split the raw flesh there. The stone glowed with a grayish internal light for a moment, then the light shifted, taking on a weird greenish cast. The green light erupted from the stone, and Gorian moved it around, beaming the light at one pirate after another. As it struck the pirates, their motions suddenly slowed, as if they fought their way through some viscous semiliquid instead of simply through the air. Their faces revealed confusion and frustration, but try as they might they were unable to break the spell.

In Gorian's hand, the stone grew painfully hot. It

vibrated with a force that he began to fear would
break his arm as he tried to hold it still. It only took
a minute to affect all the remaining pirates on the
ship, however. After that, Gorian, with a sigh of relief, released the burning fragment. Even through his
shirt, it was uncomfortably hot on his skin. The ago-
nizing sensation was leavened, though, by the ease
with which his allies disposed of the rest of the
Barachan Spur's crew. After less than five minutes,
it was done. The decks still ran with their blood but
were clear of pirates. Bodies floated in the water
around the ship. Gorian wondered casually how long
it would take the sharks to be drawn by their open
wounds, but then he turned his attention to more urgent matters.

"Now cast off!" Gorian shouted to his men. He
pointed toward the beach, where Kunios and some of
his pirates were crowding into the one lifeboat remaining there. Kanilla Rey had warned him that
magic across such a vast distance was difficult, uncertain, and could not be maintained for long. "Lose
that anchor, quick, before they reach us!"

The men, already planning for such an event, finished the final preparations, releasing the anchor
chain from the ship rather than taking time to raise it.
Until the winds caught the sails, oars would be
needed to push the ship away from the reefs and
beyond the reach of the fast-rowing pirates in their
small boat. All available hands grasped oars and set

to rowing, and Gorian looked back toward the increasingly furious Kunios with grim satisfaction.

Serving Kanilla Rey was not without its costs—but it also came with some significant benefits. In this case, life and freedom among them.

Well, relative freedom, anyway, he mentally amended. He was Kanilla Rey's man, no doubt about that. If he ever tried to break free from the hold the sorcerer had over him, he suspected he would not live very long at all.

But being one man's servant was acceptable to him. Belonging to Kanilla Rey *and* to the captain of the *Barachan Spur* was not.

Anyway, he had a job to do, in Stygia. Kanilla Rey wanted it done, so he meant to do it.

KRAL STOOD ON the deck in front of Alanya, Donial, and Mikelo, a found cutlass in his fist, while the battle raged. Best to let the mercenaries and pirates fight it out between themselves, he thought. One side or the other would prove victorious. When it did, then he would know with whom he had to contend.

When he saw the stone glowing in Gorian's fist, he immediately knew two things. Gorian was being helped by some distant mage—if he had himself been the wizard, he would have displayed powers long before now. And his side would win—the pirates were fierce, but Gorian's magic was stronger.

It wasn't until he saw wet hands clutching the side of the ship that he realized he had taken his eyes off the boat coming from shore for too long. Looking over the side, he saw that it still was too far back to provide aid for the pirates. But someone climbed onto the ship—Kral could only guess the man had swum from the smaller boat, faster than it could be propelled through the water by oar.

With a glance to make sure his friends were not in immediate danger, he started for the other side of the ship. Before he reached it, however, Captain Kunios himself swung up and landed on the deck with a thump. His eyes were wide, almost glowing with madness. He drew two swords from his belt. Water ran from him like rain, but he grinned maniacally, ignoring everything except the Pict before him.

Kral knew he would fight the captain alone. Everyone else was still occupied, in spite of the assistance provided by Gorian's magic. Besides, he had meant to challenge Kunios sooner or later, until the escape attempt and his new status as a prisoner had changed that.

Stepping forward slowly, he raised the cutlass. Kunios waved both of his through the air with swishing sounds. "You and me, boy," he said. "Is that the way it is? Fair enough. I knew we would match up sooner or later."

Kral didn't answer. He had no intention of talking

to the pirate captain. Time for conversation was long past.

He took another cautious step. The pirate did the same, his boot slipping slightly on the wet deck. Kunios was accustomed to the sea, and he regained his balance instantly. But Kral chose that moment to attack just the same. He lunged forward and brought the cutlass swinging toward Kunios's head. The pirate blocked the blow, and Kral felt the shock of contact to his shoulder.

Kunios jabbed with his other sword. Its tip sliced into Kral's ribs, but the Pict backed away before it penetrated too deeply. Kral dropped his own blade down, blocking any follow-up by the captain. Both swung again, their swords clashing furiously. Kunios kept both of his blades in motion, and Kral had to back away, parrying, occasionally nicked by slicing steel. Swords were new to him, not a weapon that Picts traditionally used, and Kunios's skill far outmatched his.

The buccaneer might have been half-mad, but he was a fearsome combatant. Kral began to wish that Gorian would direct some of his magic toward Kunios. He had managed to avoid serious injury, but had not so much as wounded Kunios.

Kunios backed Kral up, blocking, blocking. The pirate snarled and kept up the offense, his blade licking out as fast as flames from a bonfire, then drawing away, then slicing from a new direction. The deck under Kral's feet was slippery with water and spilled blood, and his heel bumped against a downed corpse. He tried to step over it. Before he dared put his foot down, though, he had to glance back to see where the body lay.

Kunios didn't let Kral's momentary distraction go to waste. He stabbed quickly, and by the time Kral's gaze returned to his opponent a blade sliced up into his ribs, not far from the previous wound. Kral let out a gasp and lurched backward, away from the blade. Blood gushed from the wound. Staggering, Kral backed up another couple of steps. But his heel slipped in a patch of blood and he went down hard.

Kunios's cutlass arced down toward the fallen Pict's head. Kral brought his own up just in time to block the powerful swing. The blow sent painful vibrations all the way up his arm to the shoulder, and he knew he was weakening. Maybe he hadn't been ready to challenge Kunios, after all.

Still, he was not about to give up. He forced himself to his feet, swinging his own cutlass toward Kunios's leg. Kunios dodged, and Kral attacked again, biting back the pain of his wounds.

And then the pirate caught Kral's sword between both of his own and knocked it spinning from the Pict's grasp.

Kral still had his knife, tucked into his girdle. But wounded, against a seasoned fighter with two cutlasses? With the ship rocking beneath his feet?

He realized at that moment that all his disadvantages stemmed from one—that Kunios was accustomed to shipboard fighting. Kral was used to forests, trees.

The closest things to trees around here were the ship's masts. Their rigging hung down like vines in the deep woods, their crosspieces jutting out like branches.

Kral bent his knees, dropped low enough for his left hand to touch the deck, and then sprang. Straight up. Extending his arms overhead, he managed to grab one of the ship's lines. Kunios charged in for the killing blow and found the deck empty.

He looked up in surprise to see Kral hanging just out of reach.

"Fine," he said with a snarl. "You take to the rigging like an ape, and I'll just have my way with your friends."

Donial and Alanya had watched the whole fight without interfering. Now Donial lifted the cutlass Kral had lost. Kral could see his arm trembling. The boy knew he had no chance against Kunios, but was determined not to fall without fighting back.

Kral would not let that happen. He had scrambled so high into the rigging that Kunios couldn't reach him with his swords. But even here, he was not helpless. He drew his knife, finally. Letting Kunios take two steps toward Donial, he released the rigging and plummeted to the deck.

As he fell, he held the knife out before him.

The speed of his descent forced it into Kunios's chest. The blade bit deep, and Kral landed on the deck directly in front of the astonished pirate. His knife was torn from his grip, remaining lodged in the pirate's middle. Blood splashed the deck.

"You . . ." Kunios said. He slashed out with both swords, coming perilously near Kral's head. Kral dodged both blades. Kunios's face was a mask of pain now, but still, he kept coming, kept raising and swinging his swords. Kral stayed just out of reach, watching Kunios's mad eyes. A line of saliva ran from the pirate's open mouth, tinted pink with blood. He tried to lift his swords, but they suddenly seemed too heavy. He released one and pawed at the knife jutting from him.

"There is a difference between cowardice and strategy," Kral said. "But it appears that you will never have the chance to learn it." He took advantage of the pirate's diversion to lunge forward. He jammed the butt of his palm against the hilt of his knife, forcing it deeper into Kunios's breast.

Kunios looked as if he wanted to say more, but his mad eyes glazed over, and his mouth went slack. He pitched forward, landing facedown on the deck. Blood pooled instantly from beneath him. Kral watched, tense, until he felt Alanya's soft touch on his arm.

"Thank you," she said quietly.

"He needed killing," Kral answered. "More than most."

"Probably," she admitted. "He would not have given up."

Kral hazarded a glance overboard. The little boat was closer to the ship. "His men have not done so either."

"Maybe if they see their captain . . ." Donial suggested.

Kral understood at once. Together, the two of them lifted Kunios's still form and carried it to the side. They held it aloft so those in the small boat could see, then hurled it out into the water. It splashed, then sank out of sight.

Still, the boat came on.

Kral had watched Gorian's magic with fascination. He saw the evident pain it caused the Aquilonian, and knew that it was a trick the man was unlikely to be able to repeat, at least not right away. If the pirates caught up to the ship, a brutal fight would ensue, and there would be many more deaths.

"Come," he said to his companions. "To the oars!"

"But . . . you're wounded," Alanya said.

Kral looked at the gash in his side, wincing a little at the pain. "That won't kill me," he said. He stripped the sash from the waist of a dead pirate and tied it tightly over the wound.

"Are you sure, Kral?" Alanya asked, concern evident in her tone.

"It will do for now. When we have left those pirates far behind, we can tend to it better."

Alanya didn't look satisfied, but she didn't argue further. Kral, Donial, Alanya, and Mikelo hurried down to the oars and found empty spots on the benches there. Without hesitation, the four of them threw their backs into the heavy work of rowing the great ship. The sails filled noisily with wind, but even so, they all knew that getting away from the remaining Argosseans would require as much speed as they could muster.

Kral gripped the wooden oar and pulled for all he was worth, bending almost double, then straightening back and arms to urge the ship through the water. His ribs screamed with pain as he rowed, but he forced himself to ignore it. As the ship pulled away from the reefs, groaning against the waves, sails cracking over-head like thunder, he could feel the sea grow rougher.

But he peered along his oar and saw that the pi-rates were being quickly left behind. The Argossean buccaneers were themselves being marooned, though on the coast of Shem and not some remote island.

"There's more to that Gorian than meets the eye," he whispered to Alanya, rowing beside him on the oarsman's bench.

"I thought that, too," she said. "I have long won-dered why they wanted to go to Stygia. Now I wonder all the more."

"As do I," Kral agreed. "And they surely wonder the same about us." He considered the men remain-ing on the ship with them. Gorian, who was in charge of the mercenaries, but had taken on the job of liberating the ship, sailors and all. Gorian's friend Sullas, who said little and stayed in the background. The mercenaries themselves, fighting men who followed the orders they were given, caring less for the reasons they fought than for what they might earn for their efforts. And the remnants of Captain Ferrin's crew, now put to work sailing a ship that was only a remnant of the one they had known for so long. Allatin yet lived, and he was the one to whom Gorian directed his commands, just as Kunios had.

A crew of about twenty, sailing a ship that would have been better served with forty at least. And that twenty included himself, Donial, and Alanya, all with little experience working a ship.

They sailed for Stygia, because that was where Gorian wished to go, and the *Restless Heart*'s sailors had no better destination in mind. Kral was happy to let Gorian be in charge, for now, as long as Gorian kept the ship headed in the right direction.

Sizing up the Aquilonian, Kral was not much impressed. The man was lithe and quick, but not particularly large or menacing. He seemed able to think on his feet, but he had waited a long time before making any moves against Kunios, and had stayed away from the fighting before that. He didn't seem to be a natural leader of men, and yet men followed him.

It was because of the magic, Kral decided. Having seen that, they obeyed Gorian both because he had led the rebellion and because they were afraid not to, lest he turn his magic on them.

Kral would wait and watch, he decided. As long as his mission and Gorian's didn't conflict, he would let the man continue in his leadership position. But if the time came that Gorian changed his mind—steering away from Stygia, for example—then Kral would have to find out which of them was the more powerful.

He believed that it was he. Gorian's magic might make him a difficult adversary, but Kral had never shrunk from a fight. He would not start now, magic or no magic. If it became necessary, he would happily challenge Gorian for leadership of this tiny crew.

He glanced over at Alanya, then back at Donial and Mikelo, rowing on the bench behind. He had not completely made up his mind about Mikelo, but the others were fast friends. Together, they would reach Stygia and reclaim the crown. Then Alanya and Donial could return to the home they had in Tarantia, and he to his village on the hill, secure in the knowledge that he had prevented tragedy from befalling the Pictish race.

On to Stygia, then. Who knew what obstacles still stood in the way of his reunion with the Teeth of the Ice Bear? Kral smiled to consider them, confident that he could overcome whatever the gods threw his way.

He barked a short laugh, and swelled his chest, letting his lungs fill with the sweet sea air. The air of freedom. His friends looked at him wonderingly, as if he had gone mad. He let them.

"On to Stygia," he said, aloud this time. "Whatever happens will happen, but I will do what needs to be done. This I have vowed, and I vow it again, before all of you."

"On to Stygia," Donial answered, tossing Kral a smile of his own.

Alanya and Mikelo took it up next, each one saying it with even more enthusiasm than Donial. "On to Stygia!"

AGE OF CONAN:
HYBORIAN ADVENTURES
MARAUDERS

Volume I:
GHOST OF THE WALL

Aided by a king's daughter and a circle of allies,
a young warrior embarks on a quest against those
who destroyed his people, and the tyrant who
took the precious Teeth of the Ice Bear.
And to do so, he must become his enemy's
worst nightmare.

He must become a ghost.

0-441-01379-1

Available wherever books are sold or at
penguin.com

In the land of Cimmeria, in the time when
Conan was King, a lone warrior battles
his own legacy—and a new legend is born.

AGE OF CONAN:
LEGENDS OF KERN

Volume 1:
BLOOD OF WOLVES

In a land plagued by an evil god, a young warrior named Kern is
destined to lead his people. But he does not know if he leads
them to deliverance—or to certain death.
0-441-01292-2

Volume 2:
CIMMERIAN RAGE

Kern must unite the Cimmerian clans under one banner—and
one army—to rid the land of the Vanir raiders.
0-441-01295-7

Volume 3:
SONGS OF VICTORY

When Kern's army has been scattered, he seeks out a
legendary weapon that can kill any man, beast, or god
in order to achieve a final victory.
0-441-01310-4

**Available wherever books are sold or at
penguin.com**

AGE OF CONAN:

ANOK, HERETIC OF STYGIA

Volume I:

SCION OF THE SERPENT

Anok Wati, a young street fighter, strikes a pact with an
ancient god—and changes his destiny forever.

Volume 2:

HERETIC OF SET

Seeking to avenge his father's murder, Anok joins the
Cult of Set and begins a journey to control the magic
that could consume his soul.

Volume 3:

THE VENOM OF LUXUR

When Anok Wati unknowingly unleashes a
hideous evil, he must destroy a god turned
flesh to save Hyboria.

penguin.com